The Phoenix Syndrome

The Phoenix Syndrome

Lucilla Andrews

HEINEMANN : LONDON

William Heinemann Ltd
10 Upper Grosvenor Street, London W1X 9PA

LONDON   MELBOURNE
JOHANNESBURG   AUCKLAND

First published 1987
Copyright © Lucilla Andrews 1987

British Library Cataloguing in Publication Data

Andrews, Lucilla
The phoenix syndrome.
I. Title
823'.914[F]   PR6051.N4654

ISBN 0-434-02131-8

Printed and bound in Great Britain
by Mackays of Chatham

I

In the ice-locked silence of the countryside in the small hours of that Sunday morning the roar of the tractor towing an open farm trailer was loud as a Sherman tank. The noise penetrated without waking the sleeping minds of the only two ex-servicemen in the Doctor's hut. Mr Hoadley East, the Senior Surgical Officer, muttered in sleep, 'I don't bloody believe it.' And Dr Lincoln Browne, the medical registrar, swung instinctively on to his face, hauled his sweat-soaked pillows over the back of his head and knocked to the floor the Army greatcoat and spare rugs over his top bedclothes. Some fifteen minutes later when he was woken by the Night Assistant Sister calling up the SSO next door, he was shivering with the cold that had filmed with ice the glass of water he had put on his bedside table at midnight.

It was two-thirty on that Sunday morning in early February 1947, when Stan, the younger of the two night porters, saw the tractor's headlights lurching in from the lane as he was using a pickaxe on the depleted coke stack behind Casualty.

'Don't mind telling you, Sister,' he later confided under his breath to Mrs Ames, the Night Sister, 'give me a real turn. Reckoned third war started up and none give us the gen.'

'Dear me, Stan, I am sorry,' she murmured, writing a hasty note at the standing desk. Casualty's only telephone was on that desk, but she was not using it for a variety of reasons that included the proximity of a fully conscious patient, his anxious employer, and the fact that it was between midnight and 6.30 a.m. and Mrs Ames was an exceptionally considerate young woman.

. The patient, a Mr Thomas Ford, lay huddled in grey Casualty blankets on a metal stretcher-trolley. He was 61 and head stockman at Widdington Farm, a large mainly dairy farm, that stood about a mile on from the foot of the east face of the hospital's hill. Tom Ford had worked at Widdington for the late grandfather and father of the slight, dark-haired young man who was standing by him and whose name was Martin MacNab. 'Sorry I couldn't give you any warning, Sister,' Mr MacNab had just explained, 'but our blower's been U.S. (unserviceable) since Friday evening's blizzard.' And a few minutes earlier he had helped Stan lift Tom Ford from the makeshift straw and tarpaulined mattress in the trailer on to the stretcher-trolley Mrs Ames held steady. It had then taken all three to push the trolley through the few yards of snow and up the hard-iced mobile ramp into the Nissen hut that for the last six years had been the Casualty Department of St Martha's-in-the-Country, the main evacuated base of the still grossly war-damaged St Martha's Hospital, London. For the last four weeks that Nissen hut had been externally converted into an outsize igloo.

Mrs Ames handed Stan the note with a comforting smile that encompassed Tom Ford under the blankets, Mr MacNab in an ex-RN duffle coat and seaboots and Stan in his old Army greatcoat, Wellingtons, and Royal Army Medical Corps beret. 'For my Night Assistant, please.'

'On the double, Sister!' Stan, an ex-corporal, didn't actually stamp to attention. He just gave that impression as he wheeled out in the cheerful certainty of being the bearer of bad news for some of the sleeping day staff. Stan had been on the permanent night staff since his demobilization leave ended last March, and had long acquired the night's traditional antipathy to the day – a tradition equally observed in reverse. Cruel time of a cruel night to have to turn out on theatre-call,

2

he mused, grinning as he stamped off a token quantity of snow at the entrance to the long, single-storey brick Administration Hut that amongst its many small offices housed that of the Deputy Matron which at night became the Night Office and base of the Night Sister and her single Assistant.

The Deputy Matron was actually the Matron of that branch and only so prefixed to mark the overall authority of THE Matron in Martha's, London, where for years, as on that hillside, the country establishment had become The Hut.

Sam Lincoln Browne woke shivering when the stealthy booted footsteps stopped at the next door on his left. He raised his head to listen to the soft knock, turning of the handle, switching on of an overhead light and quiet, 'So sorry to disturb you, Mr East –' before the door was closed. He couldn't catch the rest of Miss Yelton, the Night Assistant Sister's explanation, but Hoadley East's comments came through the dividing hardboard wall like gravelly stage whispers. 'Good God, Sister, what'll they do next? . . . belly-ache forty-eight hours . . . pain worn off . . . hard as a board? . . . suspects query perforation, eh? Huh. Right, Sister, I'll be over, stat.' (Medical abbreviation of the Latin *statim*; English 'at once'.)

Sam struck a match and discovered it was a quarter to three and why he was so cold. The stealthy footsteps faded as he replaced greatcoat and rugs, and an incoming stream of grunts, groans and blasphemies the former stage whispers. He tapped on the dividing wall. 'Tough luck, Hoadley.'

Hoadley East, hauling a third sweater over his pyjama jacket, growled, 'Sorry you've been woken, Sam. Beat this. Just had an acute 'abdo' hauled in by tractor. No wonder we win our bloody wars. So what if no ambulances have been able to get in or out since Friday's blizzard? Customers just hitch themselves up to farm tractors.'

'Think you'll have to operate?'

'Too bloody cold to think, but Prue Ames obviously does, so odds on. Get your head back down, you lucky sod of a physician,' he grunted, pulling his old battledress trousers over legs already encased in pyjama trousers and long, shapeless, white woollen operation stockings. His bed-springs groaned when he sat on the edge to put on boots. Mr East was 34, shortish, thickset, and, once his old Army greatcoat covered his long white coat, square from all angles. He slapped a pre-war tweed cap on his short, light brown hair, shoved torch and stethoscope into one greatcoat pocket, hooked the upturned collar and pulled on thick gloves before leaving his slit of a single room in what had been a wooden Army hut containing the Company Office and Guardroom before its conversion to its present use in early 1941.

The heavier footsteps had faded when Sam Lincoln Browne groped for a cigarette and stuck one in his mouth. He had been S. L. Browne in the Army and Martha's up to his call-up in mid-1941, but this last September, on appointing him as the Hut's one medical registrar, authority had insisted he add his second Christian name to his surname to avoid confusion with the current Senior Medical Officer in Martha's, London a Dr P. M. Brown. Sam disliked and kept forgetting the double-barrel, but as he had badly wanted the job – and long lost the habit of being bothered by trivialities – he would have accepted any name the top brass had chosen to give him.

It took his long thin body a long time to warm up. He was six foot one, strong-boned and now weighed a few pounds over ten stones. In late August 1945, when released after three years in Japanese prisoner-of-war camps, he had weighed under six stones. He was now 31 and had a remarkably fine facial bone-structure and well-set dark eyes, but when he struck the match for his cigarette, the flame illuminated a gaunt, yellowish face under greyish streaked dark hair that could have belonged to a frail, prematurely aged man in the late forties. He had always been thin, but the pre-war cricket sweater over his pyjama jacket hung as loosely as the operation stockings on his long, bony legs. These stockings, Dodds, the Doctors' scout from the Hut's opening, had recently taken to scrounging, from unenquired sources of his own, for those residents of whom he approved. The others either wore their own socks in bed or had numb feet. The Hut's supply of rubber hot-water bottles had dried up during the war and not yet returned; all the old Victorian and Edwardian stone bottles disinterred in 1941 from one of the forgotten storerooms in the cavernous basement of Martha's, London, were needed by the patients; and the Hut's few electric blankets were strictly reserved for patients on the Dangerously Ill List or newly post-operative. But Dodds, as he regularly observed, knew how many beans made five. He had been too old for military service in the last war, but for most of the Great War he had been a youngish gunner in France and several times a patient in military hospitals. The ex-Majors East and Browne, RAMC, always had their early tea, and, when necessary, shaving water, piping hot irrespective of coal shortages and power cuts. Dodds owned and jealously guarded an aged primus stove.

The whole country was having the most severe winter in living memory; by what some regarded as unlucky chance and others as a Higher Judgement upon the Labour Government's landslide victory in the first General Elections for ten years in July 1945, it was coinciding with a national coal shortage and consequent frequent, often lengthy, mains electricity power cuts. From shortly after Christmas, in the Hut only the wards, the Night Office and the night switch-board's cupboard of a room in Admin were kept – relatively – warm all night. Elsewhere, between 11 p.m. and 6.30 a.m., all background heating was either switched off, or where, as mostly, the origin was an anthracite stove, banked so low as to give no warmth from a yard off. The currently 298 general-bedded hospital had a few battery-powered emergency lamps and heaters, but these had to be reserved for major emer-gencies and the recent constancy of blizzards and heavy snowfalls had removed the weather from this category. The present inability of ambulances and ambulance coaches to get up or down the narrow winding high-banked lane running up to and beyond the hospital's only entrance – glorified by the title 'main gates' – was just the latest of the recent short or shortish periods when the Hut had been cut off. All over the

British mainland other country hospitals, schools, villages and some small towns were, or had been, in the same case, with all approaching lanes and side roads blocked by snow, and the nearest main roads reduced to hard-iced single tracks lined by massive, filthy snowbanks.

The Army hut encampment that had turned into the Hut had been built on a semi-flattened clearing halfway up the broader west face of the second in a line of three, highish, wooded hills lapped by open farmland some sixty miles south of London and roughly the same distance west of the Channel coast. The uncleared wood on the upper half of the hill loomed up behind the regimented line of nine long wooden barrack huts that in 1941 had been the hospital's first, and now in 1947 were its last, 36-bedded wards. When first opened the wards had just been numbered, but as the war and air attacks on London continued, the wooden wards had inherited the names of those destroyed by enemy action in the parent hospital. The line began with Charity, Ward 1, ended with Florence, Ward 9, and formed the long arm of the open oblong with tripled short arms that contained the main body of the hospital. The Army had left single short arms and Martha's had added the rest to accommodate the wartime-rationed minimum of personnel, departments and equipment vital for the maintenance of a great voluntary teaching hospital. And as around 99 per cent of the patients came down from and were returned to Martha's London in the regular twice-weekly convoys of ambulances and ambulance coaches the old barrack square had provided useful parking space and been renamed Casualty Yard when the board announcing CASUAL-TY DEPARTMENT and an old coach-type lantern with a red bulb had been fixed above the entrance to the Nissen hut.

In 1941 Martha's had put in the internal telephone system with all lines connected to the larger day and smaller night switchboards, each of which had one outside line to the local exchange. The only two other 'outside' telephones with in-dividual numbers were in the Deputy Matron's private and the Honorary consultants' communal offices. Every ward, department and staff residential hut (always called 'Home') had one telephone, but to the joy of the whole day staff a still extant wartime rule forbade the use of the Homes' telephones between midnight and 6.30 a.m. for anything but announcements of fire, a falling bomb, German invasion, or a major medical emergency. This same rule applied in reverse to the switchboard operator – one of the two night porters – to his private sorrow, as it was uniformly agreed that owing to some quirk of the accoustics the Homes' phone bells beat the fire claxons on points as, where the latter could arouse even the dead drunk, the former did that job on the dead.

All the Homes were at the lane end of the eighty-odd yard drive from Casualty. The Head Porter's little wooden lodge was on the rising right of the always open main gates, and a little higher, on its mound, was the Doctors' residence. On the opposite side, ranging downhill in parallel lines and order of seniority were the day nursing staff's Homes, then the wardmaids, and finally the communal Night Home. But from late 1942 this all-female line had been hidden from the drive by the erection on a new man-made mound of the single-storey brick Lecture-cum-occasional-Recreation Room. It was an apocryphal, but cherished Hut legend that this installation had resulted from the Sisters' profound objections to opening their blackout curtains on spring and summer early mornings and being seen in their night attire, and to seeing dishevelled young doctors shaving in crumpled pyjamas, or, it was hinted, naked to the waist. That the Lecture Room had been essential and there had been nowhere else to put it was ignored by all but those responsible for teaching hundreds of student nurses and medical students. When the Second World War finally ended on 15 August 1945, the Hut had over 400 beds, two-thirds of the Nurses Training School and eight-tenths of the Medical School. It was only last year, 1946, that the opening of the first temporary hut wards and operating theatres on some of its flattened bombsites had returned to Martha's, London, the whole Medical School, the second third of the student nursing body, and reduced the Hut's bed-state to its

7

present figure and resident medical staff from 18 to 12. This last reduction had enabled five of the vacated single rooms in the Doctors' hut to be doubled to house the ten final year medical students now coming from London on a non-stop two-weekly rota to work one week as medical clerks and one as surgical dressers. The sixth room had been left for the pathologist on call, tonight a Dr Sumner.

The torchlight on her face woke the theatre staff nurse before the whispered summons. She groaned softly and pushing aside her thick dark hair blinked in the white beam that in the darkness of the fourteen curtained cubicles of the Staff Nurses' home was blinding as a searchlight. 'Thanks, Sister. Gone to Stanley Parker (Ward 5)?'

'Yes, Nurse Carr. Being prepped and pre-medded now.'

'Theatre on?'

Miss Yelton grimaced behind the old school scarf tied over her nose and mouth. She was a newly promoted junior sister and deeply offended. Typical ex-Army type, she reflected. Obviously thought she was still coping with untrained medical orderlies. Of course she had already unlocked the theatre and turned on lights, heaters and sterilizers. Once the SSO gave the word, the Night Ass.'s routine was first the theatre, then the theatre nurses, then the Resident Anaesthetist and whoever were the junior house-surgeon and two medical students heading tonight's theatre-call list. As Caro Carr knew perfectly well! Had she been any other staff nurse, she, Miss Yelton, would have said so sharply. Only rather bad form to tick off someone who was actually eighteen months one's senior in hospital time and had served over two years as a sister in the Queen Alexandra's Imperial Military Nursing Service Reserve before coming back after demobilization last August to be the theatre's only, and the Hut's most senior, staff nurse.

Miss Yelton abhorred bad form. She compromised with a martyred murmur, 'I think you'll find all in order, nurse. Mr East has asked me to enquire how soon you can be ready and add that in his opinion Mr Ford's condition necessitates some degree of urgency.'

Caroline Carr grinned sleepily at that patently censored and embroidered message. If there's a Heaven and Hoadley makes it, she thought, he'll tell St Peter to stop messing about with the bloody book as that poor sod with the busted wing can't hang around. 'Time now, Sister?'

'Three-five and stopped snowing.'

'Okay. Tell him 03.35.'

Miss Yelton's nod was martyred. 'Him' indeed for the Senior Surgical Officer, a Master of Surgery, Fellow of the Royal College of Surgeons, with direct responsibility for every surgical bed in the Hut and who shared with the Senior Medical Officer the sole prerogative to admit. She crept away by torchlight shaking her shrouded head at the lamentable effect active service had had upon the very correct third-year who had been her night senior when she had done her first three months as a night junior in early 1943. The use of un-professional slang – and American slang at that! – would have been anathema to that Nurse Carr. Personally, Miss Yelton blamed the Americans, whom she refused even to think of as Yanks.

She had to creep in and out by torchlight when calling up theatre nurses, as to switch on their cubicle lights instantly evoked loud protests from near-neighbours. The Sisters and staff nurses had single cubicles, the student nurses, doubles, and except when being cleaned, the curtains were kept closed to enhance an illusion of privacy accentuated by the cubicles' individual french windows. During warm weather most of these were left open at night, and, now the war was over, uncurtained, which made night calls easier for the Night Ass. The only nocturnal intruders ever known in the Hut were squirrels, rabbits, cats, and, more occasionally, foxes.

The theatre had no night staff. All weekday night calls were taken in turn by Sister Theatre or Nurse Carr paired with one of the two student nurses most senior in theatre-time, known respectively as Theatre 1 and Theatre 2. All the student nurses were given three months theatre training in their second or third years; they started as Theatre 5 and worked up. Over the weekends, when alternatively Sister Theatre or Nurse Carr were off-duty, the one remaining on-duty took all night calls paired in turn by Theatres 1 and 2. No compensatory off-duty was allowed for these, or any other night calls, that, by long custom, nursing and resident staff accepted as routine events in hospital life.

Caroline Carr, switching on the bicycle lamp on her dressing-table, wasted a few seconds enjoying the shock Hoadley's language when called up must regularly cause Angie Yelton. She had been a good, if prim as they came, night junior, but, now she had a lace bow under her chin, even the halo was starched. Too bad she hadn't worked in the theatre since Hoadley took over as SSO – or was it? Angie Yelton was a gold medallist and, whatever else ailed the types that won gold medals, there was seldom much wrong with their powers of observation, thought Caroline reflectively. In 1945, for several months, she had been posted to the same newly opened British Military Hospital in the British Zone of Occupied Germany as the then Major East. They had not met before. He had been in the Army months before she entered Martha's Preliminary Training School in June 1940, but at their first meeting in 1945 he had nodded at the bronze star pinned to her QA's apron bib, growled 'Hi, Martha,' and founded their friendship that had survived a blazing, slightly drunken row in their only date a few nights before he returned to England to be demobbed just before that first peacetime Christmas, not re-meeting till last August, then working daily and sometimes nightly together, and from that date knowing far too much about each other for their mutual and individual comfort.

She sat up shivering in a thick pre-war woollen cardigan over a high-necked, long-sleeved, flannel Victorian nightgown that her grandmother had recently discovered in a forgotten attic trunk and sent from Devon to their joint ecstasy. Post-war Austerity was proving far more rigorous than its wartime equivalent. Lease-Lend was forgotten history, but Ration Books, Clothing Coupons and National Identity Cards remained essential items of British life. Even bread, unrationed in the war, was now on ration and virtually everything off-ration was either in ultra-short supply or unobtainable, off and often on, the black market.

She leapt silently out of bed and with shaking hands pulled on suspender belt and black rayon stockings before the agonizing strip necessary to hook on brassière, hitch up the shoulder-straps of the camiknickers she had made from an old nightie, and get into her waiting, grey cotton, long-sleeved, full-skirted, starched, dog-collared and cuffed, uniform dress, clean white starched apron and starched white belt. Being an experienced theatre nurse, she never wore vests on-duty. In theatre clothes, nurses were only allowed to remove aprons, starched belts and uniform shoes; whatever the outside temperature, after one longish 'op' the theatre proper was warmer than most English summer days; after a long list, it was equatorial.

The only wonder, she reflected, fixing her collar stud, is that dodging between extremes this winter hasn't flattened the theatre staff with pneumonia. Yet not one of us was hit by the new flu virus that had the first-years down like playing cards before Christmas, is still occasionally turning up and the SMO looked as if he was cooking when I ran into him on my way to lunch yesterday. He was kitted-up for Arctic manoeuvres, insisted he was just starting a cold that a bit of exercise would cure – and as he's newly married and hasn't seen his wife for a couple of weeks, it probably will.

The residents' alternate free weekends officially started at noon on Saturday and ended in time for their Sunday night rounds. Yesterday, Dr Evans, the Senior Medical Officer, and Mr Chalmers, the one surgical registrar, whose free weekends always coincided, had had to walk the three miles of deep snow that was the short cut to Pine Halt, the nearest branch-line station that was the hospital side of Ash, the nearest vil-lage. The branch-line meandered through open countryside to Arumchester, a small cathedral city thirty miles away with a good train service to London.

Ash rated as a hamlet on the map. It had a sub-post office-cum-general stores, a forge, one garage with two petrol pumps and the only taxi, an ex-US Army jeep bought by its owner-driver – no one cared to ask how – when the US Army went home, one hundred and fifty inhabitants and two pubs. One pub, the Woolpack, had two guest rooms that from 1941 Martha's had rented for the honorary medical and surgical consultants on weekend Hut call. This weekend, as for the past three, the honoraries had come down by train. They had spent the journey congratulating each other upon the wisdom of leaving their cars in London thus avoiding having to abandon them *en route* to vanish from human ken until the thaw, thereby saving the paltry extra-petrol allowance reluctantly granted those whose sole purpose was to succour the sick by those seeking to destroy the magnificent traditions of the ancient voluntary hospitals AND the British Medical Profession upon that unhappy day in the sadly not-too-far distant future. (That day was 8 July 1948, now named by Mr Aneurin Bevan, the Minister of Health, for the start of the National Health Service.)

This weekend's consultants were Dr Fenton, the senior cardiologist and Mr Armitage, the senior orthopaedic surgeon who was twenty years the younger and an ex-Lt Col. RAMC. They had reached the Woolpack just before Friday's blizzard and spent most of yesterday on either side of the log fire in the landlord's private sitting-room, smoking their pipes, drinking coffee, maligning the Labour Government in general and Mr Aneurin Bevan in particular, swopping horror stories of unpaid bills by private patients, and mutual reassurances on the quietness of the Hut and satisfactory telephone reports they had severally, morning and evening, from Dr Evans, Dr Lincoln Browne and Mr East. They regretted the unfortunate fact that not even the jeep could get up to the hospital, and agreed – truthfully – that if necessary they would foot it, but bearing in mind their own experiences as, respectively, SMO and SSO in the undamaged Martha's of yesteryear and beloved memory, few elements were less welcome to a Senior Resident than the arrival upon a Saturday or Sunday of a pundit determined to make unnecessary rounds.

*

'Theatre-call, Nurse Jones. Acute abdomen. Come along! Wake up!' Miss Yelton deposited her lighted torch on the nearside of the shared dressing-table backed against the french window to use both hands on the dressing-gowned shoulders of the fair girl sleeping face down in the left bed. 'Theatre-call, nurse,' she hissed within an inch of the sleeper's ear. 'Wake up!'

Nurse Jones heard the urgent hisses through the waves of sleep that seemed crashing against her head until she woke enough to recognize the crashing was inside and that the two aspirins that helped her get to sleep had not shifted her headache. She turned slowly, blinked painfully at the shrouded figure bending over her. 'Sorry, Sister. I'm awake,' she whispered. She was glad she had to whisper. Her throat felt so odd – not sore, just odd – that if she talked properly her voice might sound odd and if it did Pussyfoot would spot it. Pussyfoot spotted everything! She mustn't! No one must! Not till after Wednesday.

'Very well, nurse. Quick as you can. Nurse Carr's up and the SSO is waiting.' Miss Yelton played her torchlight on the untidy mound of outdoor uniform coat, rugs and top bedclothes hiding the sleeper in the right bed. 'Dress in a bathroom,' she instructed superfluously, before creeping off. Nurse Jones was Theatre 1, in the penultimate week of her theatre course and the same senior third-year set as her cubicle-mate and great friend, Nurse Kilbride, Theatre 2. They were both 21 and had to an art the technique of getting up by torchlight, gathering up indoor and outdoor clothes, boots, sponge-bags, towels, combs and powder-compacts and vanishing to the nearest bathroom without waking each other or anyone else in their twenty-eight bedded dormitory that had been half-emptied by the last exodus to London.

Never before had Patricia Jones been so anxious to achieve this and only managed through will-power. As well as the headache, her back felt on fire and legs stuffed with cotton-wool, but she as adamantly refused to recognize her own symptoms as she had to admit them to Lindsay Kilbride last night. 'I am NOT getting flu. I am NOT reporting sick to Home Sister and being packed off to Flo (Florence, the sick female staff's ward). If I just have one night in Flo, Sister Theatre'll have to alter our next week's off-duty rota and I mayn't get Wednesday. I've got it for my day off and I'm having it!'

Still unconvinced, Lindsay Kilbride insisted upon taking her friend's temperature and was only partially placated when it proved subnormal. 'Don't be daft, Pat. You look lousy. Even if it's not flu and just a cold, you mustn't take bugs into the theatre and if you are buggy and get a night-call, you'll be lucky to get off with bronchitis. Anyway, what's so special about Wednesday?'

Only because she was feeling wretched, Pat Jones whispered, 'Jock. He's fearfully upset he couldn't make last Thursday, but he's promised to visit his mother on Wednesday and I'm meeting him outside her nursing home and I'm not messing that up!' More loudly she added, 'All that ails me is that I'm pre-curse. You know I always get foul headaches and look like something the cat's brought in pre-curse. Do stop flapping and turn off that flipping light and get into bed.'

As Lindsay Kilbride knew Pat Jones very well, she shrugged, reminded herself cubicle curtains were not soundproofed and dropped the subject. Once in bed she intended thinking over what, if anything, she could do to break Pat's habit of falling hard for clottish wolves and every time convincing herself the clot was the love of her life, until a day, week or month later, she fell for the next. But the theatre had had a heavy week, Nurse Kilbride's last day off had been Monday and she was asleep within seconds of covering her head.

Sam Lincoln Browne lit his fourth cigarette since the SSO left and wondered, almost academically, how long it would be before he stopped having the old nightmares about the camps and before his first waking thought stopped being one of sheer wonder that he had come out alive. Not just out – but back to England and Martha's – alive. After sixteen months, he mused, still that same glorious wonder every morning, every time he was woken at night. He had told no one of this and amongst the other residents paid lip-service to the moans and groans about night-calls, a little because he disliked seeming to shoot a line, but fundamentally owing to his absolute refusal to discuss his experiences as a prisoner-of-war of the Japanese.

Smoking in the darkness he rejoiced again at having woken to find himself in a clean bed and neither shaking with fever, fatigue, hunger, nor anger at the latest example of bestial cruelty he had been forced to witness, and sometimes suffer, and at the overwhelming professional relief of being back in a well-staffed, well-run, well-equipped hospital. After his first few months as a POW he had been the only surviving British Medical Officer in his first and then second prison camps in the jungle. Never again, from May 1942 to August 1945, had he had one undisturbed night's sleep. Always after an hour or two, or less, 'Sorry, doc, but you said to shake you if . . . .'

One day it'll wear off, he thought. One day I'll start binding about the boring food – hold it! She's back. Full theatre call. Dick Dunlop first? Yes . . . The stealthy footsteps had stopped at the Resident Anaesthetist's door two down, right. Who else is for it? Of course, Tanner's JHS (Junior House Surgeon) heading tonight's list with those student men that switched from medical to surgical at lunchtime and from the row they all made in their party down the corridor tonight – oversize hangovers for both. Poor chaps. Rather them than me, he decided, then suddenly remembered this was Sister Theatre's free weekend. He grinned self-derisively and his mind involuntarily framed the favourite retort of a fellow POW, an Australian infantry sergeant, who had been Sam's greatest friend and the finest medical assistant he could have hoped for, and with him had come out alive. 'Save that one for the bloody Nips, cobber.'

Sam didn't notice that for the first time the mental echo of the laconic drawl only amused him and left unstirred the bottomless pit of forbidden, dreadful memories. He didn't notice as he was too preoccupied by the face that had appeared in his mind. He stubbed out, lay back, pulled the greatcoat over his face that still concealed from the undiscerning that it belonged to a young man in his prime with all the hopes and passions of his real age and that the years of enforced celibacy and the need to appear the ageless support of men older and younger than he, had drilled him into containing from others, but not himself. Being highly intelligent, he recognized the dangers of all long-starved appetites, and from his release had guarded his own. But being a normal young man there was a limit to his control upon his fantasies. He fell asleep smiling at the pale, pretty, dark-browed, hazel-eyed face in his mind at the exact moment that the owner of that face, yashmaked in a British Red Cross multi-coloured crochet shawl, emerged from the Staff Nurses' home into icy night.

The beauty of the night was as breath-taking as the sudden impact of the cold air stabbing Caroline Carr's exposed forehead with invisible needles and tightening her lungs despite the yashmak. Tonight's earlier snowclouds had disappeared. A near-full moon was high in the wide country sky that was brilliant with chinks of white frozen fire, and only Mars, low on the horizon, a red chink. The moonlight transformed the wooded hilltops into serrated mountain crests; every tree was heavy with snow, every branch, twig, fir and pine needle encased in solid ice. It was too cold for water to drip or the normal nocturnal rustlings of birds and other woodland creatures, and when, from time to time, the weight of the snow cracked off the branch of a tree, the crack echoed around like rifle fire.

Below the trees the snow softened the angular outlines of wooden and brick buildings with roofs fringed by long icicles that, where suspended above uncurtained ward windows, glittered pinkly in the red ward night lights. The wards lay on the far side of the cemented, open-sided, corrugated-iron roofed, main ramp that was just wide enough to take two full-sized hospital beds abreast; from the main, shorter, similar ramps sloped up or down to the wards and departments. Every ramp roof was smoothed white and double-fringed with icicles that at intervals were golden in the sparse ramp lights. Those lights looked abnormally bright against the navy-blue sheen of the snowlights and the darkness of so many departments. The Government was urging the whole country to save electricity and the only other outside light now left on all night was Casualty's. The head porter's lodge closed at 9 p.m. when the night porters came on with the full night staff; the night switchboard's room was their chosen base as it possessed an ancient paraffin stove that could boil a kettle and dry socks and mittens.

Nurse Carr did not need her bicycle lamp to follow Miss Yelton's deep foortmarks to the drive and then use the tractor's nearside tracks. She walked swiftly, watching her footing, whilst mentally assessing the necessary additions to the basic, sterile, emergency setting always left in readiness when the theatre proper was inactive. The Theatre Department was in the short arm that formed the left side of Casualty Yard when coming in from the main gates and directly faced Stanley Parker Ward across the main ramp. The tractor-cum-trailer had drawn up, then turned, in the broad space between the TD and Casualty, churning and streaking with oil and grime the snow that, just there, was stained crimson by the red bulb in the coach-lantern. Caroline Carr's mind was on Hoadley East's particular preference for abdominal rubber drainage tubes when she reached the churned, streaked, stained patch, and another branch cracked in the uncleared wood above. She stopped abruptly and quite involuntarily, then stared down at her snow-caked boots.

Her boots were unique in the Hut and the open envy of her peers who kept asking where she had had the luck to get them. She always said, 'Scrounged from the Yanks way back,' then changed the subject. The mid-calf boots were dark brown suede, zip-fronted, fur-lined, thick soled, and though much worn, warm and waterproof. They were the pair of US Army Nurses' issue that had been given to replace her British Army issue one night in the penultimate week of 1944. This had been after the blast of an exploding shell had blown off and ripped to shreds her boots whilst simultaneously flinging her backwards through the air and between trees for some twenty feet. She had landed on her back in a ten-foot-high snowdrift. 'Sure as hell no way to treat a limey lady,' had gasped the US Master-Sergeant who had dug her out and, finding her only badly winded, shortly, without explanation, produced the apparently new boots. 'How's for size, lady? Okay? What'da you know! Real great!' was all he had had time to say in that time and place. She had not seen him alive again, but the following day had recognized what remained of his body.

The time had been just after midnight; the place, a hastily re-formed and improvised US Army field ambulance station in a forest in the Ardennes that a few hours earlier had sustained a direct hit, killing all but two of the immediately available US medical personnel.

Caroline Carr had been one of the small British medical unit posted, at under one hour's notice, on loan to the US Third Army until their own medical replacements could be brought up. These had arrived forty-eight hours later. But, as one of the two US survivors of that particular direct hit said to Caroline in London in June 1946, when they said goodbye and for the first time used that word to each other, sometimes it took just the forty-eight seconds to hook the heart for this side of eternity.

Standing there, staring down, she smelt in memory the sour-sweet aroma of fresh-spilled blood on snow, and heard in memory the attempts at corny jokes, the weak cries 'Corpsman', the whimpers of pain and muttered prayers in long-dead American soldiers' voices and the hideous reverberations of long-silenced guns. Far clearer were the voices . . . Jeez, nurse – oh thanks, nurse . . . you a limey, lady . . . ? Oh Jesus – hold me, honey – hold me . . . ! You talk real cute – a limey . . . ? Oh, Jeez . . . oh, Jeez . . . Holy Mary, Mother of God, pray for me . . . please . . . .

She was too deep in the past to notice Hoadley East coming out of Stanley Parker then stepping sideways into shadows to watch her. He stayed in the shadows for the few seconds it took for her to collect her thoughts, shake herself physically, spraying snow from the hems of her long navy cloak and old battledress greatcoat beneath. Then she walked on more swiftly than before, round the corner from the Yard, and down the short ramp to the TD's entrance.

He did not move until the wide, wooden, self-sealing swing doors had closed behind her. He was about to follow when his attention was caught first by Miss Yelton's figure coming purposefully from the Doctors' hut and then by a second, more distant, struggling unsteadily up the incline from the Homes to the drive. Suddenly, clinically alerted, he shifted for a better view as the distant figure crumpled as if not footing but consciousness had gone. He called quietly, 'Look behind you, Sister!' and then he ran towards the dark shadow on the snow that looked so small – just then.

2

Hoadley East stepped back from the table to watch Caroline and Mr Tanner, the houseman, working from opposite sides, layer the broad, crêpe, many-tailed bandage over the still anaesthetized Mr Ford's thickly padded abdominal dressings.

'Thanks very much, everyone.'

'Thank you, Mr East,' Caroline answered for the theatre.

It was their first exchange since Hoadley's brief outline of his surgical intentions when he had come into the theatre proper to scrub up, then get into a sterile gown and rubber gloves, wearing a green linen cap and mask, white cotton vest and baggy trousers, soft rubber theatre boots and his habitual pre-op abstracted air. He loathed talking just before or during operations and for over the last hour the quiet had only been broken by his occasional 'How's he your end, Dick?' the Resident Anaesthetist's 'Nicely, sir,' the hissing of the anaesthetic machine and the soft bubbling of the sterilizers, sterile saline and water cauldrons in the semi-partitioned alcove lying off the far end of the largish, windowless, all-green two-tabled theatre. The quiet had had the unstrained quality of a small team accustomed to working together. The only newcomers were the two medical students making their first appearance as Hut theatre dressers who had backed against the nearest wall directly the op ended.

Mr Dawson, the larger dresser, was very sleepy and bored.

He had not understood what was going on and hadn't dared to ask, having been pre-warned by Mr Dunlop, the RA, not to open his big mouth if he wanted to come out in one piece. Dawson's pair, Mr Phillips – all Martha's medical students had to work in pairs in the hospital – had spent the entire op trying not to vomit and vowing himself off raw cider for life.

Hoadley, still watching his patient, grunted, 'Take him back soon as you're happy, Dick.'

'Happy now, sir.' Dick Dunlop had removed the anaesthetic mask, switched off the machine and his fingers were on the stockman's temporal pulse. 'Tough old boy, this chap. Sledge-hammer heart.'

'Glad someone's happy.' Hoadley ambled away to inspect the excised appendix waiting in a small enamel kidney dish in one of the scrubbing-up sinks. 'Nasty, messy little sod,' he observed to no one in particular.

Caroline glanced at his back, then beckoned to Stan's face that was pressed against the outside of one of the thick glass portholes in the wide, solid, self-sealing double doors. Stan hitched up his mask and swept in with the waiting stretcher-trolley. He was in theatre clothes and bristled with efficiency. A large part of his war had been spent in proper and makeshift theatres, but he preferred his present job. He had had his lot of Sister Theatres creating worse than sarn't-majors and Night Sister never created even if she missed nothing and was a real nice young lady with no side to her for all that she got the job of Matron at night and her old man been a major when his number come up.

Hoadley turned from the appendix. 'Make the home run snappy, Stan. One hypothermia's enough for one night.' He ignored the puzzled glances that evoked from all but the dressers and rounded upon the pair with what for him was uncharacteristic impatience post-op. 'Jump to it, lads! You're not here to decorate the scenery. You, Dawson! Give Mr Dunlop and Mr Tanner a hand lifting the old boy off, then help Stan ferry him back to Stanley Parker. As for you, boy –

Phillips, isn't it? Right. Get this into your wooden head, boy! Next time you feel queasy get the hell out, stat. We've enough on our minds without having to wonder when you're going to go down like a sack of coal – when we had sacks of coal – and what you'll take down with you. Our job's the patient, not scraping student men off the floor. Out, boy! Into the surgeons' room and get your head down between your legs! Out!'

Messrs Dunlop and Tanner exchanged another puzzled glance over Mr Ford's body. H.E. never blew fuses after a nifty job and he'd just done a dead nifty. Mr Dunlop busied himself helping Caroline layer Ford with scarlet theatre blankets. Mr Tanner shot out to the corridor to write on the prescription sheet of Ford's notes that the newly summoned Stanley Parker night junior held out, the short list of post-operative drugs to be given as necessary in the ward. That list, and the full operation notes that he must write in Stanley Parker before going back to bed, would be checked by H.E. on his customary, immediately post-op visit to the ward before returning to his own bed. Mr Tanner took extra care with his handwriting. When H.E.'s adrenalin was up he tore off the fastest strip in the Hut. God knew why it was up now, Mr Tanner didn't. His feet hurt too much.

The portholed doors were at the far end of the shortish, wide, departmental corridor that opened onto the ramp. The corridor's walls, ceiling and rubbered floor were the same dark leaf green as the theatre, but the walls were lined with single doors and between each, ranks of tall black iron oxygen and smaller carbon dioxide cylinders. Down the left side was a line of stretcher-trolleys in single file; on every trolley was a stack of blankets and a green linen-covered metal structure that looked like a large bedcradle and was called 'a birdcage'. When Mr Ford's trolley was in the corridor, Mr Dunlop fitted the birdcage over the patient's head and chest, Caroline covered it with a light blanket, then exchanged nods first with Stan and then Nurse Kilbride waiting by the ramp doors. The latter pulled open the doors jumping aside as Stan, grasp-

ing the headpoles, snapped, 'On the double, Mr Dawson!'
and charged off with the dresser lunging for the footpoles and
the ward nurse galloping alongside clutching notes, anaesthetic bowl and towel and bracing herself for the necessary
sprint to get ahead and open Stanley Parker's ramp doors.
Caroline watched until the trolley was through them, then
backed through the always open duty-room door to use the
telephone on Sister Theatre's desk.

'Theatre. Nurse Carr. Night Sister, please Frank.'

'Have to be the Night Ass., nurse. Putting you through to
the Night Office.'

Caroline looked at Sister Theatre's travelling-clock on the
desk. Being clockwork and unaffected by power cuts it was
currently the most reliable in the department. It was a
quarter-to-five. Odd time for Night Sister to be anywhere but
writing the full hospital night report at the Dep. Mat.'s desk.

'Assistant Night Sister speaking from the Night Office.'

'Nurse Carr from the theatre, Sister. Mr Thomas Ford, age
61, bed 5, Stanley Parker Ward has had his appendix
removed by the Senior Surgical Officer under a General
Anaesthetic given by the Resident Anaesthetist. There was
some degree of perforation and a drainage tube is *in situ*. He
has not yet recovered from the anaesthetic and has just been
returned to his ward.' She gave the latest pulse, respirations
and blood-pressure figures. 'General condition, satisfactory.'

'Thank you, nurse. I will inform Night Sister.' Miss Yelton
rang off by putting one finger down on the receiver rest, then
paused briefly to review her impatient thoughts.

Obviously, one had every sympathy for the poor man's years
as a POW, but one would have thought that experience should
have taught him not to spread alarm and despondency, that
commonest conditions were the most common, and, with this
new flu virus lingering, anyone with the classic symptoms of
the onset of an acute attack was almost certain to be its latest
victim. What was quite certain despite that silly little ninny
Jones's protestations in Cas. before the acting-SMO arrived,
was that she must have felt unwell last evening and should

have reported this to Home Sister and by now been tucked up in Flo's main ward and saved everyone a great deal of bother. Naturally, Night Sister had dealt kindly with the girl's tears – some might say, too kindly. Useless to deny there were not occasions when a little sternness was needed to help a patient pull herself together. Later, of course, Night Sister had to abide by Dr Lincoln Browne's instructions.

He was temporarily standing in for the most senior resident, as physicians took precedence to surgeons, and amongst the SMO's direct responsibilities was the health of the entire staff. Nonetheless, one would not have expected that quiet, polite, jaundiced man – tiresome condition, recurrent malaria – to throw his weight about in this fashion and one dreaded to think what the Deputy Matron would have to say about all this in the morning. . . .

She jiggled the receiver rest. 'Assistant Night Sister from the Night Office, Frank. Put me through to the Night Sister in Florence Ward, please.'

Caroline put down slowly. The theatre had to be cleared, cleaned and reset, the operation written up in Sister Theatre's log and whole department tidied before she and Nurse Kilbride left and they were due back on-duty at 8 a.m. only because it was Sunday, and this was the theatre nurses special prerogative much envied by the rest of the day staff coming on at the usual 7.30 a.m. But whenever possible, once the urgency was over, Caroline liked a couple of minutes alone to recall every detail of the op fresh in her mind. If time allowed this, she could later write it out as if taking dictation. She had mentally reached the final clip, when the electric kettle on top of one of the metal filing cabinets began boiling. She switched it off, pulled up her mask and went back into the theatre. 'Your kettle's boiled, Kilbride. Get in the mens' tea before you do anything else.'

Nurse Kilbride had just stripped the table. She dropped the last long white surgical towel into one white enamel bucket, and a red rubber mackintosh sheet into another. 'They've had to wait as the power's low, nurse,' she protested with unusual belligerence, then stormed out muttering in her impeccable English of Inverness, 'Am I to blame for a government I wasn't old enough to vote against?'

Caroline whisking her used-instruments trolley to the nearest sink wondered if there was too much carbon monoxide in the theatre air. Hoadley then Kilbride blasting off – wrong syndromes for both.

Or, perhaps not, for Hoadley. It had been a very tricky op that in less experienced hands could have had another outcome. Ford was in fine shape for his age, but that was 61. His luck had been in tonight. A less considerate boss wouldn't have turned out in the small hours in this weather, or had the Mayday in the first place. And whilst Chalmers was coming along well, he was only a junior registrar and hadn't Hoadley's six years of wartime surgery that had packed in roughly twenty of peacetime and demobbed him highly competent at general and first-class at orthopaedic surgery. He wanted to specialize in orthopods (orthopaedics) and, though the competition was cut-throat, he'd make it. He's a real survivor, not the ersatz type like me, she thought, rinsing instruments under running cold water and sorting into perforated metal sterilizing trays the 'blunts' and 'sharps'. The former, the majority, needed twenty minutes boiling before being put away, the latter, scissors, scalpels, blades, needles and so on, had five minutes.

Prue Ames is another genuine article, she reflected as her hands worked on. Prue Ames had been Sister Alexandra Ward in Martha's, London throughout the nine months of the V1 and six of the V2 attacks in the final year of the war with Germany. She had been on-duty upon the morning she heard her husband had died of wounds sustained the previous day, and a few minutes later heard her ward was about to admit more V1 casualties and stayed on-duty till evening. Major Hugh Ames, RAMC, had been Hoadley's contemporary and greatest friend in Martha's. In March 1945, a few days before their respective units crossed the Rhine, by one of those coincidences that happened in war too often to be remarked upon, Hoadley had discovered the fatally wounded patient he was attending was his friend Hugh Ames. 'Not one bloody thing I could do to save him, Caro. Just had to watch him go. How do I bloody face her with that? After all else I've blurted out?' his wine-slurred growl had spat across a small dinner-table in an on-limits to British Forces restaurant in Occupied Germany in December 1945.

'I tote a lamp, not a crystal ball.'

'Too bad you don't, girl! Might help you to glimpse what's inevitable as night following day. Your goddam Yank's a decent sod, damn him. So one of these days he's going to pack up and go home to the wife and kid leaving you with a mouthful of teeth and nothing to do but bite on the bullet.'

'How in hell can I bite on the bullet with no teeth,' she had retorted and the row had raged on.

She carried the trays into the alcove and was lowering the second into the 'sharps' sterilizer when his voice spoke her name from just behind her. She started.

'Good God, girl, what ails your nervous system?'

'Allergic to being crept up on.' She closed the sterilizer lid and set on it one of the glass-and-wood five-minute timers that, as the twenty-minute, were identical to outsize egg-timers. 'Why are you back?'

'Something to tell you. Let's get shot of this tropical rain forest.' Once in the theatre he looked around to ensure the communicating inner door to the anaesthetic room was closed, then explained.

Her hazel eyes, that theatre clothes turned bright green, darkened to bottle green. 'Jones! Exposure?'

He shrugged his powerful shoulders. 'I wouldn't have said she was out long enough. She looked a bloody ill girl when I carried her into Cas. Prue Ames was on tap. She'd heard me charging past her office window. The girl had to be warmed before anyone could take a good look at her. Prue and I dealt with that whilst the Night Ass. hauled up Sam Browne. Then I had to push off for here.'

'You had to.' She gestured to the stripped table. 'QED.'

'Yep. What gen did Prue give you?'

'Just in her one phone call from Cas. saying Jones wasn't well enough to come on, so Kilbride was being called-up, stat.' They looked at each other in the same guarded way but as they were nearly the same height and old friends and colleagues, she read the expression at the back of his shrewd, very deepset eyes. 'You think she's cooking something nasty?'

'I'm a simple bloody surgeon not a physician. I didn't like the look of her, but –' He broke off as Nurse Kilbride catapulted through the portholed doors.

'Please, Nurse Carr, Dr Lincoln Browne is here and would like a word with you and the SSO in the duty-room.' Lindsay Kilbride's voice was calm, but her eyes were startled. During the day the arrival of a full or acting-SMO on such exclusively surgical territory was an unhealthy sign; at this hour on a Sunday – ominous.

'Thanks, nurse. Keep an eye on my "sharps"', said Caroline quietly leaving the theatre with Hoadley.

Nurse Kilbride had seen the quick blank glance they had exchanged and nodded to herself. Shaken as rigid as she and Dick Dunlop to whom she had been handing over the tea-tray in the doorway of the surgeon's room when L.B. came in from the ramp looking like one of the starving survivors from Stalingrad in his navy woollen tea-cosy hat, greatcoat and boots. Though she and Dick had both been holding the tray at that moment, it just missed being dropped.

Pat? But all Pussyfoot had said was that she was a little unwell and to get weaving stat as the op was about to start. Yet, if not Pat – why come to the theatre? And if Pat – still, why? Even if the daft wee clot had the double pneumonia she had been asking for – and that wasn't all after letting herself get picked up on trains, but away with her love-life just now! This clearly meant some flap on somewhere and there'd be another if those 'sharps' boiled to a jelly.

Lindsay Kilbride re-tightened the waist-tapes of her gown and having enhanced her resemblance in theatre clothes to a smallish, padded, wasp-waisted green bolster on flapping black-galoshed feet, bustled into the steamy alcove.

Florence Ward stood at the highest point of the main ramp that, a few yards on, ended at the hospital chapel in another Nissen hut and behind which was an old footpath running up through the wood, over the top of the hill and down its steeper east face. Florence was the only ward in the Hut with four, single-bedded small wards off the short wide corridor between the main general ward and ramp doors. The small wards had hardboard dividing walls and front curtains – another unique feature. In all the general wards fixed-footed screens were used to screen individual beds. Nominally, Florence's small wards were reserved for Sisters, but always used for patients on the Dangerously Ill List, or suspected of, or suddenly developing, a notifiable infectious disease. Being a general hospital the Hut was forbidden to treat such diseases that once diagnosed had to be transferred to the nearest appropriate Fevers Hospital. And in the varying time it took to effect these transfers the patient was 'barrier-nursed'.

Barrier-nursing was one of the routine techniques taught to all the student nurses and had much in common with the strict no-touch-technique (which meant as said) used in the theatre and surgical wards. The infectious patient was constantly screened, nursed in stringent isolation by masked, gowned staff and after the patient's use, every article was either boiled, stoved, soaked for twenty-four hours in strong carbolic solution before being laundered, or burnt. The need to barrier-nurse for shortish periods was fairly common in Martha's, London, but rare in the Hut owing to its geographical isolation and the numbers of admissions first examined in the parent before reaching the country branch. Consequently, the Florence night senior had been astounded when a call from the Night Ass. in the Night Office told her to prepare Small Ward 1 for the immediate admission of Nurse P. H. Jones requiring barrier-nursing and to deal with this on her own. 'Your junior must remain in charge of your main ward and have no contact with Nurse Jones, nurse.'

Only a little later the newly gowned night senior's mask had hidden the mingled interest, curiosity, and apprehension in her face when Nurse Jones's stretcher-trolley was wheeled in only by Night Sister and the acting-SMO. But being, as all the present night seniors, in the third-year set two to junior Nurses Jones and Kilbride and on her third spell of three months night-duty in the last two years, she was not surprised when, about thirty minutes later, Dr Sumner, the pathologist on call, joined Night Sister and Dr Lincoln Browne behind the drawn front curtains of SW1.

A few minutes after hearing Mr Ford was back in Stanley Parker, the two physicians left Florence and walked slowly, in silence, down the main ramp. Dr Sumner, a slight middle-aged man whom a chronic gastric ulcer and myopia had exempted from military service in both world wars, was muffled in tweed hat, two scarves, and heavy pre-war over-coat. He walked with his head down, shoulders hunched, and under one arm the wooden box fitted with test-tubes, test-bottles, glass slides and other items without which no Martha's pathologist was ever seen around the hospital. Now in that box were the nasal and throat swabs and blood samples he had just taken from Nurse Jones. And still in silence they stopped at the junction with the side ramps to Stanley Parker and the TD and in unison looked up and down the line of snow-shrouded wards with the fluorescent pink frosting the outsides of the uncurtained windows and blocking any glimpse of shadowy white beds.

Dr Sumner covertly glanced up at Sam's face. They were standing just under a roof light that caricatured the angularity of high cheekbones and strong jaw and gave the taut skin the texture and hue of an old lemon. Dr Sumner sighed inwardly. He well recalled the extraordinarily good-looking young registrar in London in '41 whom he had first encountered as a pre-war medical student. Bad show. More than malaria had left its mark. Very bad show. All over now, mercifully, but only too understandable the poor chap refused to discuss it and that others had done so on his behalf and consequently gained him his present appointment. Far from easy, that last. Only two demobbed chaps as yet had their feet back on the

Hut's residents' ladder, only a handful in London. Up there, Martha's, as every teaching hospital in the UK, was swarming with demobbed chaps from the medical branches of the Services taking refreshers or post-grads to acquire the higher qualifications that might enhance their prospects of finding employment. Slender prospects, alas. For every medical vacancy currently going in this country there were long, highly qualified and experienced queues. Any chap lucky enough to have an appointment, reflected Dr Sumner, needed to walk warily. One slip – dozens eager to replace him with good war-records ten a penny, if not, be it admitted, many from his show as too few had come back alive. Nevertheless, he needed to watch his step and it would be distressing to see him blot his copybook thus prematurely. Not that there was any question that he knew his medicine. Always shown great promise. Qualified with Honours in Medicine and obtained his Membership before call-up. However, whilst it was wise to avoid reliving the past, it was less than wisdom to ignore the facts that the past formed the present and that a chap accustomed to accepting as daily events fresh cases of typhoid, dysentery, diphtheria, black water fever, pellagra, malaria, gangrene – to name but a few – might have lost sight of the merciful fact that such conditions were not frequently encountered in the clean air and isolation of the English countryside. Unarguably, the situation varied in Martha's, London. The unusual was continuously manifesting itself – as was inevitable in all great cities – and especially the odd case of diphtheria in autumn and winter as the condition was endemic in London, again as all great cities. Admittedly the sick girl had visited London for her day off last Thursday and the incubation period fitted, nevertheless. . . .

Dr Sumner cleared his throat. 'As I have already stated, Dr Lincoln Browne, in my opinion you are most prudent and entitled to back your early diagnosis in the manner you have just so succinctly outlined to the good Night Sister and my humble self. However – er – I trust you will forgive the observation that should bacteriological confirmation prove inconclusive, or – er – lacking, those in high places may not be best pleased by your Draconian methods. You – er – have not considered consulting Dr Fenton?'

'I'll ring him at breakfast time, sir. I can see no advantage to Nurse Jones or Dr Fenton in getting him out of bed at this hour. He can't give an opinion until he sees her; getting him here must take time and time isn't on her side.'

'Quite so. But my point –'

'I have taken it, sir. Thank you for making it.' Sam spoke slowly, as if making the mental translation from a foreign language as that was how he had felt whilst the pathologist was speaking. Do you seriously think I give a damn about such hot air in this set-up? Sam had wondered, then answered himself. Of course you do and how else could you think after spending your entire working life in Martha's, where what-the-pundits-say is regarded as Holy Writ. It's irrational and unfair to expect you to understand what it was like to have to diagnose with a stethoscope – only with luck a thermometer – and otherwise just your own eyes, hands and experience.

He went on, 'I stick by my diagnosis, sir. I agree her throat is not yet typical, but her general condition looks to me very typical of the early stages of dip (diphtheria). If I'm wrong, I'll wear it,' he added with a determination in his low voice and gaunt face that was new to Dr Sumner but would have been immediately recognizable to two former Japanese Commandants of Allied POW camps had not both since been hanged for War Crimes.

Dr Sumner blinked up over his glasses and brushed aside his frozen breath hovering like ectoplasm and clouding the lenses. 'I shall join you in the Theatre Department shortly, Dr Lincoln Browne.'

'Thank you very much, sir.'

Dr Sumner had not arrived when Sam waited in the duty-room whilst Caroline and Hoadley briefed their respective juniors. After the cold outside the cramped little duty-room was a gentle oven heavy with the mingled smell of anaesthetic, ether, carbolic and cigarette smoke. Sam had left his greatcoat and tea-cosy draped over oxygen cylinders in the corridor. He wore a pristine long white coat over several sweaters topped by a black woollen rollneck, a pair of pre-war black cords over his pyjama trousers and aside from his boots and overnight beard he looked neat enough to be starting his first morning round. He already had the reputation of being the Hut's neatest resident, as amongst his legacies from captivity was a personal fastidiousness that was to be with him for life.

He sat smoking and thinking deeply in one of the two hard chairs facing, across the small flat-topped desk, Sister Theatre's chair that Caroline had just vacated. His thoughts were purely professional but he was aware of the measure of surprised relief he had just been afforded by the discovery that Caroline Carr spoke his language. He had expected this of Hoadley, not her.

'Poor lass. This'll put the cat among the pigeons,' had been Hoadley's immediate reaction.

And Caroline Carr's, 'Poor kid. I am sorry. Did you know she was on-duty up to nine last night, doctor. . . ? Yes, Night Sister would have told you . . . no, none of the theatre nurses have early evenings on Saturdays. Either we have ten-to-ones or two-to-fives. Yesterday Jones had the first, on Friday a two-to-five and Thursday was her day off. . . . Yes, she went up to London – sorry, I don't know why in this weather. . . . No, I'm ashamed to say I didn't notice anything unusual about her yesterday. . . . Oh yes, wore a mask all day, we live in them in here, and now I think of it, she was rather quiet, but if I had noticed – then I'd have thought her just browned-off by all the extra cleaning we have to do on non-list weekends. Browns us all off.' She had paused a moment. 'I suppose you know her cubicle-mate Nurse Kilbride is on now . . . ? Yes, you would, but do you also know they are great buddies? You'll want to talk to Kilbride, but may I before. . . .

Caroline came back first leaving Nurse Kilbride in the theatre sitting upon the anaesthetist's high stool as Caroline had insisted before breaking the news and asking what had to be asked. 'Take five, honey,' she ended. 'No hurry now. You won't be coming back on-duty this morning. I'll make us tea soon as the men clear off and Kilbride, I really am very sorry about this.'

Lindsay Kilbride knew she was from that 'honey'. Carr only used it when something got her down and Lindsay guessed she had caught it nursing Yanks in the war. Once she had asked this and Carr had laughed and said, 'Probably.' When Lindsay later handed this on to Dick Dunlop over a canteen coffee, he said it was too bad none of the other Hut staff nurses had been dragged from the convent to put in two years hard amongst the brutal and licentious soldiery and that he'd lay a month's pay that the other reason why Carr was the only human staff nurse in the joint was six foot deep somewhere in Europe. 'Sticks out a mile, Lindy. She's buddies with all us chaps and she couldn't care less about any of us. Why else would a popsie with her smashing face be unhitched at 27 and have chosen to lose rank and spend her working life behind a mask?'

Maybe she should talk to Carr over tea? But what could she say? Lindsay's pretty grey eyes stared unseeingly into the steamy alcove. It was not just that she had promised Pat never to breathe a word – she knew so few words. She didn't know the clot's real name, where he lived exactly – though it must be near as they'd kept dating – and she only guessed he was married through Pat's being so hush–hush about him. She wasn't positive – not POSITIVE – Pat had seen him since he stood her up in London last Thursday. But if Pat had not seen him, how could she have known he was going up to town next Wednesday and shooting this line about being miserable over standing her up. Miserable? Tell that to the Marines! He was giving Pat the run-around only the wee clot didn't see it –she never had seen it – and what she, Lindsay, could do to that clot 'Jock' now, didn't bear thinking! If he was a Scotsman, he was a disgrace to Scotland, as but for him Pat wouldn't have horsed up to London and picked up dip. All her talk of a para-hunt had just been eye-wash for the rest of their set and worked as she had come back with a beauty. And dip, unless L.B. had gone haywire and Carr was sure he hadn't. And dip, thought Lindsay tensely, could be a killer, especially to little kids. What if he had kids? How do I know? Och, away, I'll have to spill the beans and trust Carr. Pat'll want to kill me – and so'll I me if some kid in Ash comes out with it next week –och, no!

Suddenly, belatedly, she recognised her own position, as she had stopped flapping about catching bugs from patients in her first-year. But as she was now within a few months of State and Hospital Finals and had had all her Fevers lectures, the colour ebbed from her flushed masked face and she had to close her eyes.

'A para-hunt?' echoed Sam sitting down again oppsite Caroline. 'Sorry, Nurse Carr, I'm lost. She just told me shopping.'

'That's right,' Caroline sat straight-backed, the mask round her throat, hands in green lap, and green turban pushed a little back to heighten her high white brow and Sam's impression of a young nun forced by her vows to ignore the sexuality in her sweet-lipped mouth and soft, slightly husky voice. 'It's a hunt through ex-Army surplus stores for parachutes. They don't need clothing coupons, have masses of lovely soft silk and every prospective bride in the UK is out for one for her trousseau. Only way she can get one. Some are dyed a ghastly yellow, but the best are cream. Jones got a cream for one of her sisters who's marrying this June from some place behind Victoria Street.' She had spoken as if giving a medical report and in the same tone added after a brief pause, 'Kilbride's never had dip nor been immunized. She'll be 22 in May.'

'I see.' He looked down at his lighted cigarette and missed the expression that flicked through her eyes. Neither said more until about a minute later Hoadley East returned.

'Dunlop's in the clear. The rest, sitting ducks.'

He sat heavily beside Sam, absently accepted a cigarette from the squashed, blue-paper wrapped packet Sam held out, and looked at Caroline. He had shed gown and cap, but still had a mask round the neck of an aged Fair Isle sweater, and baggy cotton pants tucked into theatre boots. 'Kilbride?' She shook her head. 'Bloody hell. Right. Dick, you and I cleared, so lets get cracking on the nuts and bolts.'

'And start praying no more acute abdoes roll up on tractors before Tuesday afternoon.'

'Amen to that,' intoned Hoadley, and Sam, watching both, understood much that had previously puzzled and occasionally disturbed him.

At the ramp end of the corridor Dick Dunlop took his time closing the surgeons' room door after the SSO. Dick was 23, sturdy, brown curly-haired and engagingly amiable. He was in his second six months from qualification and leaving this May to start two years National Service. In the May of 1945 he had been one of a large body of final year medical students from London's teaching hospitals working in Belsen Internment Camp in Germany very shortly after its liberation by the British 2nd Army. Belsen then had a major typhus epidemic, but diphtheria had been endemic and Dick had there seen more of typhus, diphtheria, and far, far worse, than he could bear to recall. Being well-balanced, he had recognized the horrors of Belsen would haunt him for life and trained himself into consciously blocking out all moments of recall. That mental discipline demanded its own time. It was a few seconds before he closed the door and turned smiling to the trio of young men sitting round the spartanly furnished room's one small deal table. Messrs Tanner and Dawson were lighting fresh cigarettes. Simon Phillips was slumped in a hard chair, arms folded, eyes closed, still cursing himself for having hit the cider so hard at last night's medical students' stag party.

'Okay, chaps. Get scrounging handbells and UNCLEAN labels, necks for the use of.'

Mr Tanner frowned. He was a well-built, quite attractive young man – his mother thought him Robert Taylor's double – and newly qualified. He took his short white coat and himself, seriously. 'No joke, Dick. Hell of a bind having to sit around on our backsides waiting for old Sumner to swab us and line us up for Schicks.'

Paul Dawson's healthy red face was bemused. He was 21 and had only managed to scrape into the Medical School because his father was an old Martha's man. He liked being a medical student as it let him go on playing rugger that much longer. He never listened in lectures. Some other chap always did and let him use his notes. Just now he had only taken in one in three of the SSO's spiel, but if he could spit out the odd term at home the old man might raise his allowance. 'Who's this Schick when he's at home?'

Mr Tanner grasped the chance to display the medical knowledge that he thought should have earned him a first job as a house-physician and not lowly house-surgeon. His mother thought him a genius.

'Schick, Dawson, is the standard pathological test for the individual susceptibility to diphtheria. Jabs in both forearms. One's the test, the other the control. But!' He slapped the table and Simon Phillips shuddered. 'Takes at least twenty-four hours and often longer to get a correct reading.' He explained why in pedantic detail. 'Ergo, L.B. can't possibly know yet if the wretched girl's got dip. Sumner hasn't even had time to turn up the Klebs-Loffler, so –'

'Come again?'

Dick put in, 'Roughly, old chap, the Klebs-Loffler bacillus is the bug that causes dip. The dodgy little swine lurks in the nose and throat but, being dodgy, isn't always easy to find first go, and sometimes, second.'

Mr Tanner looked pained. 'Actually, he's right.'

'We gasmen know our fevers,' said Dick airily and ostensibly investigating the contents of the teapot, temporarily lost the thread of Tanner's continuing lecture on the signs, symptoms, treatment and possible complications of diphtheria. '. . . adds up to the plain fact L.B.'s gone off at half-cock making a diagnosis on clinical grounds and damn all else. At this stage her clinical symptoms must be similar to acute flu, an acute strep (streptococcal) throat, Vincent's Angina, and rows of other possible differential diagnoses.

'If you ask me,' he insisted to the now punch-drunk Paul

Dawson, 'the chap's clean round the bend bunging us into quarantine, closing this joint for fumigation –'

'Martha's statutory rule, Bob,' interrupted Dick, 'after the known presence in the TD of anyone incubating or developing a notifiable disease.'

Tanner ignored this. 'I suppose its inevitable the chap'll always be halfway round the bend after letting the Japs nab him.'

'He had a choice, Bob? MO's are non-coms (non-combatants). Non-coms don't bear arms. MOs in the bag couldn't try for an escape. Couldn't leave the chaps minus an MO on their side. MOs were in for life or the duration, whichever ended first and, but for the atom bombs, the first for L.B. The Japs never kidded any that, come the Allied invasion of Japan, they'd bump off every service and civvy Allied POW in their hands. Men, women, kiddiwinks – kaput.' Dick sliced a finger across his throat. 'Some choice, chum.'

Bob Tanner flushed with impatience, not embarrassment. He was fed up to the back teeth with the war that had been an hideous bind and ahead was a worse, National Service. 'I only meant L.B.'s bound to be a bit touched. That's obviously why the pundits let him jump the queue and shoved him down here for quiet and clean air. Actually, I feel sorry for the poor chap. I'll bet by this time tomorrow Evan Evans and every pundit in the old firm is out for his blood.'

'How much, Bob?'

He hesitated. Dick's knack of backing winners was notorious. 'You must be joking!'

'Not so, but far, far otherwise. L.B. *is* going by the books. Read 'em up. The early diagnosis of dip should be made on clinical grounds as sooner the antitoxin's bunged in, better the chances the poor bod won't go out feet first. Ergo, chum, were I acting-SMO right now, I too would have hauled up old Sumner and the yellow (quarantine) flag and dealt sharpish with this and that. Dip's incubation period is one of the shortest in the business. The swine shows up from one to six days from contact and most often on the second to fourth. If the popsie did pick it up Thursday, all Friday, all yesterday, she was back on the job oozing bugs.' Dick smiled smugly around the table. 'Having had it in prep school, you lot may drink with impunity from my cup. And though you chaps,' he told the dressers, 'have missed out on direct contact with our Nurse Jones, if I were you I wouldn't let poor old Bob breathe all over me.' He turned to Tanner. 'How are we feeling, old chap? Any dryness in the throat? Twinges in the back and legs? Little chap with the hammer going into action behind the eyes? Not to worry! You'll know the worst in a few days, if not sooner, and if you have missed out on the first round and are Schick positive, positive – remember him telling you you need the negative, negative to be in the clear, Dawson? – not to panic, Bob! Old Sumner's Passive Immunization shots'll have you in the clear for a good two to three weeks. Natch, Active Immunization would do that job for a few years but as it takes so long to get working, PI's the one for emergencies. Okay, chaps.' He rubbed his hands. 'My ten bob's on L.B. . . .Who's on?'

Paul Dawson brightened. This he understood and he had only met Dick Dunlop when his batch came down from London on the Saturday before yesterday's.

Mr Tanner took no part in the bet. He was too occupied in taking his racing left radial pulse under the table.

3

It was a little after ten on Monday night when Caroline returned to the empty Night Office after her first night round of the quarantined nurses. She rang Frank, on the night switchboard, to say she was back before taking off crochet shawl and old battledress greatcoat, but not her cloak and boots and relighting the two paraffin stoves. As she sat down in the Deputy Matron's chair the lights went out and both telephones started ringing. Cursing indiscriminately the government, miners, electricity company and local swans, she groped for the receivers in the faint flickering flames of the old, black cylindrical stoves standing on tin trays on the floor at either side of the impressive leather-topped mahogany desk long salvaged from the ruins of the Hospital Secretary's London office. And forgetting the Deputy Matron was left-handed, she spoke first into what she assumed was the black internal receiver in her right hand. 'Night Office, Night Ass. speaking, Frank. Emergency, or can you hold?'

A professional operator's distant voice demanded, 'Are you the Night Sister in St Martha's-in-the-Country near –'

A second, distant but hoarse, male voice broke in, 'The Night Assistant Sister'll do, thanks, operator. Sister, this is Dr Evans from London. I'll hang on whilst you find out what Frank wants.'

'Thank you, Dr Evans.' Caroline changed mouthpieces. 'Night Ass., Frank –'

'I heard, Nurse Carr. Give me time to light me candles. So you got the SMO on your outside. I got Home Sister for you from the Sisters' Home. Ask her to hold?'

Angie Yelton, thought Caroline, covering the blue mouthpiece. 'No. Through now, please.'

'Righty-oh, nurse.' Frank pulled out and pushed in plugs and switched on his 'operator's' voice. He loved the night board. Kept him warm as toast and rested his corns lovely. 'Through to the temporary Night Assistant Sister now, Sister.'

Home Sister was long over retirement age and had volunteered to stay on for the war, and since, until a replacement could be found for her unpopular and mainly domestic job. Her quick voice remained youthful. 'I do hope you'll forgive my being a little unethical, Nurse Carr. I was looking out for your return from your round up here but missed you in the darkness. My night vision is not quite what it was. But before retiring for the night I should like to know how they all looked to you.'

Which means, honey, you don't like the look of Angie either. Nothing less would make you cut red tape. 'Sister, I thought all the student nurses looked very comfortable and showing only minor reactions to their injections, but that Miss Yelton's seems much more acute. I've just given her the prescribed sedative and will look in on her hourly. I've not yet had time to report this to Night Sister or Dr Lincoln Browne, but I'll be bringing him up to see them all once he finishes his night rounds of the wards.'

'These reactions invariably vary with the individual, Nurse Carr. Some patients find them most disturbing.'

As the thought in both our minds, honey. 'Sister, after Dr Lincoln Browne's round of the Homes, would you like me to call in if your cubicle light is still on?'

'I shall be awake and most grateful if you would, Nurse Carr. Many thanks, my dear.' She rang off.

Caroline's eyes had grown acclimatized to the flickering, shadowy darkness. She put down the black and spoke into the blue receiver without bothering to light the trio of candles in tin holders on the desk. 'Still there, Dr Evans?'

A bout of coughing prevented him from replying but not from appeasing the operator's demand for 'another one shilling and nine pennies, caller!' He fed the coins into the black metal box of the public telephone in the front hall of an Edwardian terraced house just off the Bayswater Road where his wife lived and that he shared on alternate weekends. Their double-bedded bed-sit on the fifth floor had a hand-basin, gas-ring and gas fire; a kitchen and bathroom shared with their landing; the rent was five guineas a week (£5.5s). Dr Evans salary was £20 a month, all found; Mrs Evans, an ex-ATS sergeant now secretary in a City office, earned £6 a week.

'Sorry about that, Nurse Carr,' he gasped eventually. 'Must be you as it's your voice. Before my last lung consolidates, what are you doing in the Night Office and what did Frank want? Make it snappy. Not just to save my bankruptcy. From the trouble I'd getting this trunk call through any moment they'll cut me off. You'd think there was still a war on.'

The Dep. Mat. hadn't heard it was over, thought Caroline. Yesterday mid-morning as *ad nauseam* during the war. . . . In these trying times, Nurse Carr, we must all do our bit. Please be in bed by three this afternoon and report for duty as Miss Yelton's temporary replacement tonight. . . .

Caroline gave Dr Evans a short, censored reply. Yesterday morning Mrs Evans had rung the Hut with the news that her husband had woken with a temperature of 103.8, diagnosed himself as flu, hoped to throw if off in a day or so and till then couldn't return to duty. Tonight after her handing-over report, the Dep. Mat. said his temperature this evening was 102.4 and from his voice, cough and breathing now, it was higher.

'How are you feeling, honestly, doctor?'

'Feverish and frustrated. One solitary bright spot. I'm not a dip. Had it in '28, the year before I picked up the tubercle that kept me out of the war. How about you?'

'No, but Schick double negative as –'

'Your dip was undoubtedly one of the unexplained feverish illnesses you had in childhood. So TD still closed?'

'Yes' she said, relieved his impatience had saved her explanation that the Active Immunisation she had had in 1945 was still in date. In the late spring and summer of that year in Occupied Germany she had nursed scores of the living skeletons newly liberated by the Allied Armies from the German concentration camps. Only a few had spoken enough English and had the strength – and weakness – to talk of their horrific experiences. None had said much. Just enough to leave lifelong scars in her own and Hoadley East's memories, as Dick Dunlop's. None of the three had ever talked of this to each other, or others.

She went on, 'Surgical Stores set up the twenty-four-hour fumigation this morning. Couldn't start yesterday as only one man on and its a two-man job. The TD'll re-open at one tomorrow afternoon and pro tem Sister Theatre's standing-by to use Cas. as an emergency theatre which we're all praying won't be necessary.'

'I'll add my prayers. Sister had it?'

'At school.'

'Inevitably. Never ceases to raise its ugly head in educational establishments and will continue to do so until some government has the sense to insist upon immunizing all children under five, workers in such establishments and all non-Fevers Hospitals. Why our own erudite establishment does not' – again his cough stopped him and heightened his annoyance at missing one of the most academically interesting situations to have occurred in the Hut since he took over as SMO. He was a good, kind, conscientious physician, but, as the majority of those reaching his present post, an ambitious man. The recognition that Sam Lincoln Browne's speedy and correct handling of this matter must place him in the kind of limelight that would do no harm to his professional future, was no antidote to an acute attack of flu. 'That takes care of my remaining lung,' he spluttered. 'Hold it. More pips.' He pushed in more coins. 'There, nurse – good. I'd hoped to catch Mrs Ames on the Dep. Mat.'s private number for the full picture. Aside from the tactful version you've just doled the patient, all that I got from L.B.'s short call last evening was that Nurse Jones' dip had been pathologically confirmed, the local MOH (Medical Officer of Health) notified, and the snow was holding up the Jones girl's transfer to Badgers Heath Isolation Hospital – understandably seeing it's ten miles the other side of Arumchester. She still in Flo?'

'No.' She heard and was smitten with guilt at the genuine concern in his voice. She should have guessed he would spot the kid gloves and that knowledge would do less damage than ignorance to a sick but very responsible SMO. I've been in the theatre so long I've forgotten that any physician that's good at the job is far better than the average surgeon at seeing through brick walls, she registered rapidly. Surgeons see the bricks very clearly, but only the exceptional like Hoadley sees what lies beneath and on the other side. 'She went this morning. The Rural District Council hired from somewhere an old US Army bulldozer and two tractors that cleared the way at different stages. Tonight's report from Badgers Heath was, quote, Nurse Jones is comfortable and as well as can be expected, unquote.'

'There's an original report! And the general view remains that she caught it in London on Thursday?'

'General hope.'

'We can but hope. Any obvious suspects?'

She was now prepared to give him the truth, but not un-proven hunches. 'Bit early to say, doctor.'

'Not all that early. Specifically if she didn't get it in town and the Hut's now harbouring an unsuspected "carrier". She could be the start of the first wave. Quarantined being checked four-hourly?'

'Yes. And there isn't a throat in the Hut Dr Lincoln Browne hasn't looked at since yesterday and the Path Lab looks about to go under swabs for the third time.'

'They have my sympathy. Total bed-state still 291?'

'292. We had in an acute abdo.'

'So you did. L.B. told me.' He had to put in more money. 'I'm sending a bill for this to Martha's. Why shouldn't I

43

have my cut before Nye Bevan collars all our loot. How about this week's convoys?'

'Temporarily postponed. The official version, owing to the weather. The patients due for discharge tomorrow and Thursday are being splendid. Dunkirk spirit in every ward.'

'Not that there'll be one without the inside gen – damn this cough!'

She waited till the bout subsided. 'Shouldn't you go back to bed and take a swig of linctus, Dr Evans?'

'Don't give me that old Physician Heal Thyself. Getting enough of it from my wife!'

She had been a long time in the theatre, but before, for much longer, a bedside nurse. Often in a ward, humour worked where tact failed. 'I was merely thinking that as you sound ready to decide on oak or elm, you'll be that much easier to measure in bed.'

He laughed. 'I insist upon brass handles.'

'I should hope so. Oh!' The lights had come on. 'Thank God.'

'Why the gratitude to the Almighty?'

She told him. Then, 'Too short for a cut. Must've been a swan.'

'A – WHAT?'

'Swan. They've wide wings and will fly into cables.'

'Now I know I'm delirious. I shall crawl back to bed. Thanks for the gen, Nurse Carr. Have a quiet night.'

'And you, doctor –' but he had rung off.

Reflecting upon unproven hunches she made a note of his call on the memo pad that was a dog-clipped stack of strips from the blank backs of old, used, temperature charts, then noticed the strips were even thinner than during the war. It could still be on, she thought, replacing her fountain pen in her dress bib pocket, so its a bit unfair to blame the Dep. Mat. for forgetting it's over. She's still having to box-and-cox her trained nursing staff that's already so stretched that if we are in for a dip epidemic, God alone knows how we'll cope. But, as Mrs Ames said when we left the dining-room to come on tonight, 'We'll cope, somehow, as always. I hope you got some sleep today, Carr, as I'm afraid you're in for a lot of route marches in the snow tonight.'

'I slept well, thanks, Sister,' she lied, unsuccessfully, from the particular quality of the smile it evoked in Mrs Ames sweet, chubby fair-skinned face. They had not worked together for years, but Caroline immediately recognized that especially placid smile as for three months in 1943 she had been senior day student nurse and Mrs Ames the staff nurse in an officers' orthopaedic ward in one of the Government's Emergency Medical Services Hospitals with a large loaned Martha's nursing unit. Prue Ames was then recently married and Dr Ames the Hut's SMO, but though Mrs Ames was a Silver Medallist, she had been transferred to the EMS from the Hut when she returned from honeymoon. The war had forced the Matron of Martha's to abandon the tradition – now creeping back – of demanding a nurse's resignation upon marriage, but then – as still – the Matron refused to allow married couples to work in the same branch of Martha's.

Caroline was still sleeping in her own Home, but owing to her fellow staff nurses' consideration, all day it had been quiet as the Night Home. It had taken her hours to get to sleep, as her mind had kept turning over and over Lindsay Kilbride's reluctant disclosures over tea in the theatre duty-room in the early hours of yesterday.

'I just had to spill it, Nurse Carr. He must be a local. If he's been in contact he could spread it all round Ash – and if he's married there's his wife – maybe kids – but I honestly don't know if he's got any. I don't know for sure he's married or that she'd seen him since Thursday and – and I don't know what to do.'

'Nor do I, right now, honey. So little to go on. Let's take this one step at a time. The first is to wait for the bacteriological confirmation, though I'm afraid I'm certain that's coming. Then I'll have to think and somehow keep the covers down. Don't ask me how as I don't know yet.'

Roughly ninety minutes after that conversation, at twenty

to eight, Sam rang Dr Fenton over the honoraries' outside line in their communal office. The local telephone exchange was in Ash, opened at 8 a.m., closed at 9 p.m. and in the interim all local lines were put through the much larger and so anonymous Arumchester exchange. The three young women working in shifts on the Ash exchange lived and had been born in the village, were known by name to most of their callers and took a friendly helpful interest in their work and never hesitated to pass on free messages to Mrs X, Mr Y, or Miss Z if out when rung, or to explain why they were out and where they had gone.

Sam talking to Dr Fenton substituted for 'diphtheria' 'Klebs-Loeffler'.

Dr Fenton, aware the landlord of the Woolpack was in hearing, said impassively, 'I shall be up as usual this morning, doctor. There appears no improvement in the elements, so I shall suggest to Mr Armitage we embark at nine. How far the jeep can transport us remains to be seen, but I trust we will be with you by ten o'clock. Thank you, Dr Lincoln Browne.' He rang off.

Sam did the same shrugging mentally. Old Ferdie Fenton normally addressed him as 'Sam' or 'Browne'. Too bad, he thought, rushing back to his room to bath, shave, change, and with luck have breakfast before his appointment with the Dep. Mat. . . . Mrs Ames had promised to fix this for eight-thirty. On his way out he ran into the three Office Sisters coming on-duty for the day and from their frigid greetings knew the grapevine had flashed the news to the whole day staff at breakfast. Make a change from binding about cold breakfasts on Sunday, he thought, giving the Lecture Room an appraising glance as he went up the ice-packed cemented steps to the Doctors' hut. Just the job for the quarantined's daytime base if he could swing it. Could? Scrub that – would.

He was re-dressing when Dodds knocked, came in, and without preamble volunteered to take on the extra job of running the Lecture Room for the purpose in Sam's mind. 'I reckoned you'd be wanting to use it, Dr Lincloln Browne, sir. You name

46

it, I've had it. Dip, scarlet fever, typhoid, dysentery, trench-fever, measles, chickenpox, small – no! There you have me, sir. Never had the smallpox and never had the mumps.'

Sam smiled slowly. 'Dodds, you're slipping and thanks very much. You've just read my mind. Being able to say you're willing to take it on will help twist arms.'

Dodds lined face creased in a rare, dour, smile. He hadn't much time for the Dep. Mat., starch all through, he reckoned, and had most the nurses and his lads (the residents) shaking in their shoes. Not this lad. Give better than he got when he had to, he would, being a nice quiet proper gentleman. Dodds minded the nice quiet proper gentleman he'd served in the first do and when it come to fighting clean or dirty, you couldn't hold a candle to any. 'The Deputy Matron'll see it your way, sir. Not saying she'll like it. Not a one to take kindly to change, she isn't, but she'll see it your way. Have to, seeing as you're wearing the SMO's cap.' He watched Sam buttoning a clean poplin white pre-war shirt. 'Be wearing your hospital tie today, sir?'

'Nice tip. Thanks.' Sam put away the waiting dark grey and took out the old Martha's tie that he could not recall last wearing. During his five years absence from England it had been stored with his other civilian clothes, books and personal possessions in the attic of his old parental home near York that from mid-1943 had been the joint inheritance of his elder brother's young widow and small son. 'I'm afraid this extra job'll be a bind to organize. They'll have to eat there. No dining-table.'

'You're wrong there, sir, but being newish down here you'd not be knowing. The old ping-pong table and trestles the student lads used to put up weekends when we had the Medical School is still under the platform. Just need a bit of elbow grease. I'll fix it, sir.'

'Fine.' Sam knotted his tie. 'All their food, crockery and cutlery'll have to be taken up and the last two kept there and by some means sterilized after every use.'

Dodds nodded. 'Reckoned as much, sir.' He produced a

folded form from the breast pocket of his blue linen jacket. 'I've written out a chit for two of those old fishkettles Surgical Stores got on their back shelves. Do a treat on my primus. I'll have the one for a sterilizer and its mate for heating up the food. Tidy step from the main kitchen. And that pantry over the way –' He jerked his white, near crew-cut head at the window overlooking the drive. 'It's got a sink and draining-board but no cooker. Got a plug for a kettle, mind, and the old kettle's still there. I'm not saying it's not seen better days but no call to fetch up Repairs and Works. I can fix it. If you'll just sign here, sir.'

'Gladly.' Sam signed. 'No end to the wonders of modern science.'

'If you say so, sir,' allowed Dodds, removing himself and leaving Sam to finish dressing and reflect upon the British genius for improvisation and muddling through when the chips were down. Promise nothing but blood, tears, toil and sweat and the lot ganged up behind you singing 'Rule Britannia'. Promise them Utopia tomorrow, as the present Labour Government, and either half came out on strike or couldn't be bothered to show up for work, so no coal got dug out of the ground and the whole country ground to this near-halt.

Daft as brushes, Nanny Bunbury would have said, he mused, as the associations with his tie had stirred memories of the long dead Yorkshirewoman, who had been the adored nanny of two small boys until, at seven, Sam followed his elder brother to preparatory school. Or not at all daft but paradoxically illustrating that innate common sense the rest of the world regularly wrote-off as a combination of arrogance and stupidity? The war had drained the whole country financially, physically and emotionally; it was still as ex-hausted as any patient after a long, dangerous illness; after such an illness convalescence was essential and needed time, if there was to be full recovery. As if the old order, like the centuries-old phoenix, had burnt itself out on the funeral pyre of the war; the ashes had to grow cold before the new phoenix rose again. Signs and symptoms of collective and individual onsets of that syndrome now omnipresent in the UK, though I've only just spotted it. Now I have, the present national set-up makes dead sense; if Utopia's due to show up tomorrow, what better time for taking it easy and having the good lie-in than today?

He had finished dressing and putting on a clean white coat gave his appearance a cursory check in the long strip of mirror a previous occupant had illicitly nailed to the back of his door. Being a Sunday, and as the Dep. Mat. and Dr Fenton were indelibly indoctrinated by Martha's traditions, he had on his only good suit, a dark broadcloth made by his late father's London tailors in late 1940. He had first worn it when taking his MRCP in 1941. It now only fitted across the shoulders and the trousers needed a belt as well as braces, but the open white coat concealed most of the suit's looseness but not its elegance. He looked better than tidy this morning. There was no sign in his newly shaven face that he had had less than three hours sleep. There was a new vitality in his dark eyes, that, with a new hint of natural colour beneath the sallow yellow, for the first time suggested at the prematurity of the greying streaks in dark brown hair that had recovered its former thickness and a trace of healthy sheen. He noticed none of this, but had he done so, would have just been mildly amused. He had no personal conceit. He had been the least handsome and least favourite of his outstandingly good-looking parents' two children, but as his parents had greatly loved both, and Sam them and his elder brother who had returned his love, Sam had accepted second-place as his natural order before shedding his milk teeth. By the time he started in Martha's, his patent oblivion to the fact that he had been the best-looking man in his year and arguably the whole Medical School, had caused his peers first to forgive and then forget it.

His thoughts were back on Nurse Jones's rather pretty and very determined young face turned greyish, tear-stained, sunken-eyed and white-patched round the mouth. It had

taken him a long time gently to coax out her symptoms, and
how she had spent her off-duty in the last six days. She had
insisted that aside from the day trip to London, she had not
been off this hill. 'Just to the top for walks, doctor . . . I like
walking in the snow . . . No, just me – makes a break getting
away from the herd. . . .' He had recognized she had been too
ill to dissemble, yet throughout his clinical instincts had sensed
she was holding something back. As these were only instincts
he had not mentioned them to Mrs Ames, who had been present, or anyone else. Later, in Flo's duty-room, Mrs Ames had
said, 'I think the poor child had told you all she can pro tem,
doctor. Poor little thing, I know just how she's feeling. I'm so
glad I could tell her I had it at her age in my first-year – we
had to be 21 to start training then – only dropped to 19 in '40
– and when you know you're cooking something ugly it does
help to have at your bedside living proof that you can pull out
of it and pick up where you left off.'

He had hoped Nurse Kilbride might enlighten those instincts and drawn a blank. 'Oh yes, doctor, I know for sure
the only time she's been right off this hill was last Thursday
. . . No, not for these last two weeks . . . Yes, she often spends
her days off down here as her home's in the north. Trains are
so ghastly, especially in this weather and you can't bike on
this snow . . . No, I'm certain she hasn't been into Ash all
week. She likes pottering up our wood, but whose feet are up
to the six-mile round hike in the daily three hours off . . . ?'

And Caroline Carr, 'I'm sorry, but I can't tell you any
more about Nurse Jones's movements than you've just had
from Nurse Kilbride. I wish I could be more helpful, but I
can't.'

Later, when he had left the TD with Hoadley, momentarily
Sam's mind had strayed to the new insight afforded by his
first opportunity of seeing Hoadley and Caroline together, on
their own with him, in the kind of professional moment that
coming as it had in the pre-dawn hours, ripped off the starch.
'Brighter type than she looks, Caro Carr.'

'Good protective cover being a glamour girl,' had grunted

Hoadley and neither had spoken again as they trudged on, heads down against the cold, to the now lighted Pathological Department that lay parallel with the TD on the other side of Casualty Yard.

The ringing of the telephone that was on a wall shelf in the corridor between the SMO and SSO's rooms, interrupted Sam's reverie. He heard Dodds taking the call and ringing off. A second later Dodds knocked and came in. 'Just an Office Sister to say eight-thirty'll suit the Deputy Matron, sir.' He looked at his watch. 'Cut your breakfast a bit fine, sir.'

Sam grinned. 'Get it after. More appetite.'

Dodds looked him over and smiled dourly. 'If you say so, sir.' And what I says, he added mentally, is give us another month or two of feeding you up son, and there'll not be a nurse in the Hut not setting her cap at you. Shot in the arm being minded you know how many beans make five and if old Ferdie don't like it he best watch his step and I best keep an eye out in the lane for that jeep.

It was a quarter-past ten that morning when a telephone call from the Head Porter – prompted by the reconnoitering Dodds – had Sam, Hoadley and their attendant housemen waiting at the main gates when the two honoraries struggled on foot up the remaining yards of lane, having left the jeep in a snowdrift at the foot of the hill. Both men were heavily mufflered, overcoated and booted, and beneath wore black professional jackets and pin-stripes. Each carried a black leather medical bag; Mr Armitage wore a tweed cap of similar vintage to Hoadley's and Dr Fenton an even more aged black astrakhan hat given him as payment for a bill by an impoverished White Russian private patient.

Hoadley murmured, 'Both coronaries imminent.'

Sam slightly shook his head. 'Got to relieve Stalingrad first.'

He had been so late for breakfast that Sister Dining-Room had averted her disapproving face to avoid having to wish him 'good morning'. He was even later for the final serving of lunch, but her indulgent, openly proprietary smile was identical to those he had been collecting since noon from Dr Fenton, the Dep. Mat., and every ward Sister, staff nurse and houseman on the medical side. The whole of Florence was now closed; isolation notices were going up like bunting; and Dodds had lit the anthracite stove, put up the old ping-pong table and installed fishkettles and his primus in the Lecture Room renamed by the entire staff, the Leper Colony.

Caroline picked up the black receiver. 'Where have Night Sister and Dr Lincoln Browne got to, Frank?'

'Night Sister's just left Stan Parker for Henry. Dr Lincoln Browne's in with the nippers. (Martha, the ward for all children under nine.) Who'll be first, nurse?'

'Hold everything.' She heard the stamping of boots in the entrance to Admin that was some ten feet from her closed door. 'Someone's coming in. I'll ring you back.'

'Righty-oh, Nurse Carr.'

She put down before the knock on the door and called, 'Come in,' hoping it was Hoadley looking in to say he had finished his rounds and was going up to his room. The surgical side was quiet tonight, and this could give her the chance to tell him that neither Home Sister nor she liked the look of Angie Yelton and ask him to tip off Prue Ames and Sam L.B. in person which would be preferable to giving this over the switchboard, the fount of the night grapevine. Frank viewed his job as an operator exactly as the girls on the Ash exchange.

'A very good evening to you, Staff Nurse, and please forgive this intrusion.' The slight, black-haired, smiling stranger in the doorway pushed off the hood of his duffle coat and gestured apologetically at his seaboots. 'Sorry to expose you to a Force 8 but if I step inside I'll wreck the cuddy's carpet.'

She was only momentarily surprised. She stood up smiling politely, inwardly amused by Prue Ames's descriptive powers and relieved by an item of Ash history that had begun flashing round the grapevine within a couple of minutes of Sam's notification telephone call to the local MOH yesterday. 'Good evening, Mr MacNab of Widdington Farm, isn't it?'

'Stone me! Brilliant! Yes, I'm Martin MacNab. How did you do it, Staff Nurse? Radar?'

She shook her head smiling. 'Mr Ford, of Bed 5, Stanley Parker Ward told me early this morning that you were ex-RNVR and would probably call in some time today unless your phone was mended and from his ward's day report I knew he'd had no visitors or phoned enquiries during today. You'll be glad to know from that report I can tell you Mr Ford has had a reasonably comfortable day and is doing nicely.'

His well-bred English voice thanked and again congratulated her warmly, then launched into a long account of how he had just berthed his tractor in the lane and how relieved old Mrs Tom, young Dora, the Fords' war-widowed daughter, her sprog Steven and his wife Marigold would be when he got back to good old Widdington with the wizard gen.

And whilst he talked his dark blue eyes openly undressed her.

Caroline listened with the expression of unwordly gravity that had proved invaluable when nursing Mr MacNabs – and she had nursed hundreds. Just as Prue Ames said last night, she observed 'the slight, dark-haired type of knockout who's marvellous in a crisis and whose roving eye will still be roving at his last breath which he'll use to power his pass at the nearest young woman.'

Mr MacNab, now eyeing her more quizzically than lasciviously, reiterated his gratitude to the Hut. 'But much as I'm enjoying this meeting, I mustn't keep you hanging about. Bound to be most frightfully pushed what with – er – one thing and another.'

She heard the new concern in his voice, but for more than ethical reasons had no intention of helping him out unless she had no alternative. She disliked the types that patently expected her to take the visual strip as a compliment. 'Hospitals are busy places, Mr MacNab.'

'Are they not! Particularly –' he hesitated then smiled disarmingly. 'May as well come clean. Thing is, Staff Nurse, most of my chaps at Widdington live in Ash and they seem to have picked up some gen about your having the odd case or two of diphtheria – if so –' He waved both arms. 'Not to worry over yours truly or old Tom, or come to that Mrs Tom. We all went down with it when it hit Ash way back in – when was it? – '32 or '33 – in the water or something. You knew?' Caroline nodded. 'By God! MI5 must look to its laurels.'

'The diphtheria epidemic that decimated Ash in the winter of 1933 is hardly a Top Secret, Mr MacNab. You were saying –?'

'Yes, yes, where was I? Of course, Marigold – my wife – she hasn't had it, nor has young Dora, her sprog or our young Nick.' A different and very attractive smile illuminated his very Celtic face. 'Ten months and the hell of a good chap is young Nick.'

She did not have to like him to like his paternal pride and responsible attitude to his own and his employee's family.

'Congratulations. Your first?'

He laughed. 'Number Three. Two more chaps away at prep school. You see before you paterfamilias, and weighed down, so straight question. Diphtheria aboard?'

No alternative now so she gave the officially decreed reply, 'Unfortunately, yes. We have had one case, a member of staff, now transferred to Badgers Heath Isolation Hospital. Fortunately, she had no direct contact with any of the general wards during her infectious period, nor, to the best of our knowledge did she in that time visit Ash. All members of the staff working with her during that period have been pathologically tested and those without immunity to diphtheria have been immunized and are being quarantined for seven days, to be absolutely safe. 'Dip,' she went on less formally, 'Appears in one to six days from contact. In addition, the department where she worked has been closed for fumigation and the exclusively sick-staff ward to which she was admitted before transfer, closed for seven days. That means no admissions, discharges, or visitors. The hospital hasn't been closed and we're all hoping that won't be necessary and she'll prove an isolated case, but –' she hesitated, 'by Wednesday, the next "visiting afternoon", the picture may alter. After what you've just told me, personally, I wouldn't advise Mrs MacNab or Dora to visit Mr Ford. Mrs Ford's different.' She smiled faintly. 'You can only get dip from direct contact – one break.'

His expression quickened briefly. 'That's what I thought and why I insisted I, and only I, did the recce up here tonight. Thanks a lot for giving me this straight and, may I say, so kindly. You're dead right. Neither my wife nor Dora must come near this establishment until the final "all clear". Young Steven's four.' He frowned. 'Same age as Dora's only brother when the poor sprog bought it in '33. Black day at Widdington, that. I hope this poor nurse that's caught it does all right. Any idea how she's doing?'

'As well as can be expected from this evening's report.'

'Good show. Any idea how she got it, or aren't you allowed to say?'

'Still an open question though the probability is in London last Thursday on her day off.'

He dropped his gloves. He bent down quickly, and when he straightened the depth of the flush on the healthily tanned face of an obviously fit man in the mid-thirties accustomed to physical work, struck a disturbing note in Caroline's mind. She looked at him thoughtfully and said calmly, 'We are all hoping she will make an uneventful recovery and be back with us in a few months. Before you go, Mr MacNab, may I ask you something?'

His disarming smile re-appeared. 'Anything, Staff Nurse. Any time.'

'Have any of your boys been immunized against diphtheria? If not, you and Mrs MacNab should think about it, and suggest Dora does the same. As you remember the Ash epidemic I needn't explain why.'

'You couldn't be more right and I couldn't agree with you more.' He paused for thought and as she was watching him closely she saw the odd mixture of anxiety and relief flicking through his expressive eyes. 'Snag is, my wife's dead ag'in jabbing sprogs. Took old Doc Yardley and me all our soft-talk to get our trio vaccinated. Old Yardley's our local chap. The Yardleys have been pill-pushers in Ash long as the MacNabs have raised the Saltire at Widdington. My great-grandfather was the first. Long ways from Sutherland.'

'Very.' But in your case, only when you speak. 'Please forgive my pushing this, but it can be a life-saver. Couldn't you use more soft-talk on Mrs MacNab?'

He nodded gravely. 'I must. You're dead right to push it as – sorry, as this you haven't mentioned – but if this nurse didn't get it in London isn't there a chance that – what's it called – there's a "carrier" around?'

She had hoped to avoid this one. Not just a knockout but so on the ball that maybe I'm maligning you, she thought. She said, 'That possibility hasn't been overlooked, but – and this is just my opinion – I think it more possible than probable as we're so isolated, haven't had a previous dip since the Hut opened, the local MOH says the last in his area was over three years ago, "carriers" have to pick it up from someone and don't "carry" indefinitely without passing it on. Of course, there always has to be the first case and more than that I truthfully can't say.'

'You couldn't have been more helpful. May I have the honour of knowing your name?'

'Nurse Carr.'

The instant recognition that evoked in his eyes re-struck the note much more loudly. 'How do you do, Nurse Carr?' He bowed. 'If you want to know how I do, it is infinitely better than when I opened this door. My lucky night!'

'Lucky?' she echoed off-handedly being too preoccupied by her own thoughts even to hear someone else coming in from Casualty Yard.

'My dear Nurse Carr – what man in his right mind wouldn't think himself lucky when running into Hedy Lamarr in a staff nurse's uniform?'

She looked at him with the expression Dick Dunlop labelled

'betwixt thee and me stand my vows and the convent grill' and the surgeons' room agreed froze a chap solid at fifty paces. 'Thank you for calling, Mr MacNab. I'll tell Mr Ford and am sure he'll be pleased and would like you to give his love to his family and regards to Mrs MacNab.'

'I shall, indeed! Please return the signal and many more thanks,' he replied with the practised charm of a man knowing when and how to make a quick retreat. 'I couldn't be more grateful! Goodnight Nurse Carr.' He backed swiftly and straight into Sam who for the last half-minute had been standing unnoticed about a yard behind him. 'I say, sir, do forgive me! Just casting off! Goodnight, sir.' He hurried out.

Sam watched the outer door close before turning to Caroline and pulling off his tea-cosy. He stifled the urge to ask why she had just shot down the chap for being bang on target and the effect her lovely unmasked face, framed by the neatly upswept roll of dark brown hair and crowned by the small starched lace, back-bowed cap, was having upon him. 'MacNab? Should I know him and why was he here, nurse?'

She told him the truth but not what she suspected was the whole truth, as, if her suspicions were correct, there was no longer any danger of Jones having given him dip or his spreading it. And if this proved Jones as big a fool as Kilbride suspected, she, Caroline, was the last person to pick up a stone.

He had come in, closed the door and unbuttoned the greatcoat he had bought in Australia this time last year for his return by sea to England and the English climate. As all those released from his and many other prison camps in Malaya, Burma, the Dutch East Indies and Japanese mainland, he had been taken for treatment in an Australian hospital, and given a long sick-leave before being repatriated. This was partially as Australia was nearer and the ex-POWs had urgently needed medical treatment, and partially, said not only the British Army grapevine – as the physical conditions of the majority had been too horrifying for immediate exposure to their families and the British public. The photographs and reports of their imprisonment in the British press and on the newsreels in late August and September 1945, had sent a tidal shock-wave of horror and anger over the UK and caused the reports and pictures of the results of the atom bombs on Hiroshima and Nagasaki that had begun appearing in the second week of that August to be largely dismissed either with, 'Hideous weapon, but nothing else would have stopped the war. Pray God one never has to be used again;' or more commonly, 'The Japs started it attacking Pearl Harbor without even declaring war – they asked for it, they got it, and after their barbaric cruelty to our chaps, our women and our kids in their hands – too bad President Truman hadn't a third up his sleeve.'

Sam said, 'I thought I knew his face. I've seen him driving a farm van up and down our lane. Frank says you were asking my whereabouts. Why?'

'I don't like the look of Miss Yelton.' She explained why succinctly, and liked his quietly friendly manner and way of listening. It had not occurred to her to think of him as a friendly type before, on the rare occasions when she had thought of him. He had been just a man she had seen around the Hut, particularly over Christmas when, as ever, from Christmas morning to Boxing night the whole hospital was in party mood and whole staff on-duty, and she had had for him the particular sympathy she had for all ex-POWs. The return to civvy life and their private dreamworlds that no longer, and probably never had existed, was tough enough for most of the demobbed, but tougher still for the ex-prisoners who had had too much time for dreaming, too little food, too little hope, and had had to live in captivity in the knowledge that they had either been forced or ordered to surrender. The civilian public had warmly welcomed their return, but not all the men ending the war as active servicemen had shared this attitude. She had never forgotten a time in the final weeks of the war with Germany when, in the bomb-ruined outskirts of Hanover, she had seen a newly liberated, tattered-uniformed, pale-faced body of British ex-POWs being driven in a convoy of open lorries through a British regiment advancing in battle order on either side of the road. The men in the lorries had waved and whistled. The marching men had watched the lorries cold-eyed and not one had waved or whistled back. 'Can't blame the lads, Sister,' had said the RAMC Staff-Sergeant sitting between her and the ambulance driver. 'Most this lot been slogging it out years whilst that lot,' he had jerked a derisory thumb at the vanishing convoy, 'been sitting it out cushy waiting for us to open the gates.'

Having now given her explanation, she added, 'I could be flapping. She could just be having an acute reaction to the shots.'

'Or the shots as easily confusing her other symptoms. If she is starting dip the shots were too late to prevent it, though they should help lessen the severity of the attack. Let's take a look at her.' He took her coat and shawl from a hook on the back of the door as the black telephone rang. He smiled. 'Inevitable.'

The smile she returned as she raised the receiver, raised his pulse-rate. Easy, cobber, he cautioned himself, bloody easy. A few seconds later the caution was superfluous. 'Mr Dunlop from your mess for you, doctor.' She held out the receiver. 'He doesn't much like the look of two of the chaps.'

The quarantined men were Messrs Tanner and Mathers, another JHS, Simon Phillips, Paul Dawson and the two medical students who had been theatre dressers on Friday. The men, and Miss Yelton, were still sleeping in their own rooms, using bathrooms strictly reserved for them, and, as all the quarantined, had been told to avoid all contacts outside their number, spend their days in the Lecture Room and take any exercise in the hospital grounds but well away from wards and ramps. The five student nurses isolated were the four from the TD and the Florence night senior who had admitted and nursed Nurse Jones on her first night. The following night the Henry day staff nurse, immunized by dip in early childhood, had taken over Florence at night. The five nurses had been moved into the now otherwise-empty Fourth-Year Home, and the very few fourth-years in the Hut were in previously empty cubicles in the Sisters' and Staff Nurses' Homes. Miss Yelton remained in the Night Sisters 'flat' in the Night Home (two small single bedrooms and shared bathroom), and, until she started feeling really ill tonight, in a seething impatience with the wretched ninny Jones for causing this kerfuffle, the burden it was already placing upon the Deputy Matron that might yet – one had to face it – add another upon THE Matron. Useless to pretend that even Martha's, the great St Martha's, was not suffering from the shortage of young trained nurses now affecting just about every general hospital, large and small, in this country. Miss Yelton blamed the Government. She could have told them what would happen when, in July of last year, they lifted the old wartime ruling restricting the movements of civilian nurses. Of course it had happened! Thousands had resigned from the profession to marry, or rejoin their demobbed husbands and start families, as anyone with an atom of sense would have realized since nurses' working hours and the concomitant necessity to live in, were incompatible with marriage. It had been just as obvious that once free to choose where to work, thousands more would take posts in the Dominions and the United States where – one had to face it – nurses' working hours, conditions and pay were vastly better than those in their homeland. Thousands had gone overseas and were still going immediately their training ended and one could only wonder how the wretched Mr Aneurin Bevan thought he was going to have enough nurses to staff his National Health Service hospitals – only one wouldn't wonder about it just now as one's headache was being a trifle tedious. . . .

Sam put down. 'Mathers and Phillips.'

Her eyes widened. 'Phillips? Already? He's had no contact with Jones. He swore blind he didn't even know her by sight. Isn't it too soon for him to have it from one of her contacts?'

'Nothing's medically impossible. But –' he shrugged, 'I'd say the last is unlikely.'

She said evenly, 'Then he must have got it from the same

source as Jones and his hangover's been confusing the issue, and we must have a local "carrier".'

'Not necessarily. Not knowing what Jones looks like he can't know whether or not he's run into her around the Hut in these last few days. Only takes a few moments to hand it on in an enclosed area like the inside of a doorway. Everyone runs into everyone else all the time on this hill, though the cold's cut down there, but a big ally now. Masks the runners-up. Let's see 'em first then sweat if we have to.'

His common sense was reassuring. 'Maybe Dunlop's flapping too,' she said, removing her cloak to put on the coat, then replacing the cloak and adding the shawl.

He did not answer immediately. She was yashmaking her face and he thought how the crocheted colours enhanced the whiteness of her forehead, darkness of brows and lashes, and Hoadley's comment on her particular protective cover. 'Unlikely either he or you are. Ferdie Fenton told me yesterday how much dip you and Hoadley, and Dick elsewhere, ran into in '45.'

Her eyes aged visibly. The only person to have told her privately that Dunlop had worked in Belsen, was Sister Theatre. 'Hoadley hadn't –?'

'No. I'll put out the fires.'

'I'll brief Frank on us both.'

It had started snowing since he had come in and the flakes slanted by the opened Yard door. 'Wouldn't you know it?'

'Hold everything.' She backed to the stand behind the door and pulled out a faded red-and-yellow golfing umbrella that had belonged to her father who had died of pneumonia when she was 18. 'Big enough for both.'

'Let's have it, then it won't take my eyes out,' he said smiling as if upon a social occasion.

She smiled back and their eyes exchanged the mutual understanding that this was one of those moments that were too serious to be taken so outwardly. And as they went out into the falling snow she suddenly recalled how incomprehensible had been this very English attitude to the gentle, intelligent

US Army physician of French-Spanish stock who had been her greatest friend as well as her only lover; frequently, in the early stages of their relationship he had been shocked, sometimes angered, by her habit of papering such a moment with a laugh, or corny crack . . . oh my lovely honey I surely know you are not one cold-blooded bitch but right now that is surely how you sound. . . .

The snow fell steadily, silently, covering the tracks of the one ambulance that had come and gone in Casualty Yard today and the coach-lantern cast a serene crimson pool on the smoothed whiteness. They left the drive to plough through the deeper snow on the uneven downhill slope to the Night Home and stayed silent until she stumbled and he caught her round the waist to stop her falling. 'Thanks, buddy. Hear this –' She looked up at his shadowed face under the sheltering umbrella. 'Much more in this outfit and I'm doing a Captain Oates.'

He laughed and they ploughed on in silence.

4

The six, corridorless coaches of the 1.05 p.m. Saturdays only
to Arumchester were waiting at Pine Halt when the hospital
van dropped Caroline and Sam before taking the non-resident
part-time cleaners home to Ash. The cleaning ladies shouted
farewells as the van backed out of the station yard that was
slushy as the roads and lanes still surrounded by snow-covered
farmlands and hills. It was the second Saturday after the
Monday night when Miss Yelton, Mr Mathers and Simon
Phillips developed diphtheria and on the following morning
the MOH closed the Hut until seven days without a fresh case.

The patients took this news in the spirit they had the
convoy's initial postponement and agreed amongst themselves
that dip was a mite nastier but common as the measles and
like the old bombs if one got your number you'd had it so no
sense fretting. And no denying the wards weren't a sight
warmer than home what with the weather and power cuts
and trying to get a bit of heat in the hearth wrapping coal
dust in damp newspaper to burn slow – if you'd the luck to
have the dust left in the bunker and could lay hands on a
paper. What's more, in the wards you got the three meals
regular and the cuppas afternoons without you, or the wife, or
the woman next door, having to queue hours to fetch something on to the table that, what with the meat ration being
the one-and-tuppence a week and real eggs just the one a

month, was most like to be one of those nasty tins of snoek (a South African fish) or a bit of that nasty whalemeat that Dr Edith (Dr Edith Summerskill, the Minister of Food) was always carrying on about and anyway, worse things happened at sea.

The general reaction of the staff was equally pragmatic. The war had subconsciously conditioned even those too young for active involvement into accepting bad news as expected events and leaving tomorrow's problems to tomorrow. It had been a long war; it still cast a long shadow. Dip was an ugly, agreed the staff, if not as ugly as TB that messed up your training or qualifying by keeping you warded for years and who couldn't reel off the names of student nurses and medical students that had had to drop out with TB? What was a few months off with dip against that? And as for Mr Chalmers' luck in being told to stay home until out of quarantine or he got the plague – some were just born lucky. And what was so new about being holed-up on this iceberg of a hill? Bound to be holed-up months as the Path Lab hadn't turned up the 'carrier' who must have handed it to Simon Phillips – but scrub that! Get this! The gen is the SMO's got double pneumonia – my dear, yes! Left lung collapsed! And the only reason why L.B. isn't officially SMO is Sister Flo! I had the pukka gen from – who had it from – and it seems Sister Flo went through the roof after L.B. made Martha's history by shoving men into a women's ward – yes, I know they went into small wards but if Flo isn't female, what is it? So Sister Flo complained to the Dep. Mat. officially – yes, my dear! – wanted it on record that she's running a womens' ward and not a bawdy house – as if poor little Mathers and Phillips would have known what to do surrounded by all those mirrors and red plush even if they hadn't been feeling like the Wrath of God. . . .

In the event, there had been no further cases, nor 'carrier' found. The four in Badgers Heath were reported as making slow, but steady progress and foreseeably to be discharged in around six weeks for at least two months sick-leave. When the Hut officially re-opened this last Tuesday, Dr Evans had returned from an uncomplicated attack of flu and Mr Chalmers from a trying week's holiday. His conscience had forbidden his leaving the house or seeing his girlfriend, his mother had moaned non-stop about rationing and queuing and his father about telephone bills and the Labour Government. On Tuesday morning Caroline had been taken off nights, and for that night replaced by an Office Sister and from the following a junior Sister had arrived from Martha's, London and taken over as the new, permanent, Night Ass. . . . Caroline had been due for three nights off, but she had been requested – as the British Army was requested to volunteer, i.e. 'you, you and you' – to return to duty in the TD at 2 p.m. on Wednesday, and have one of the two owing nights tacked onto her next free weekend and the other to her next holiday. She had responded as anticipated, as whilst mentally cursing authority she had recognized it had no alternative since, for this week only, convoys were due on Wednesday and Thursday mornings and the back-log of 'cold' cases would have the TD going all out. Before Wednesday's incomers were in their new beds, the Hut was back to normal and containment of the dip outbreak forgotten hospital history. Few in the country branch bothered to congratulate themselves or those concerned for the escape from what could have been a major epidemic, but in Martha's, London, several in high places privately agreed upon their own wisdom in appointing a medical registrar who had demonstrably not forgotten all the medicine they had taught him and was worth keeping in one's mind's eye.

This was both Caroline and Sam's first free weekend for three weeks, but neither had known the other was going to London till they met at the main gates to wait for the van with the little group of head-scarved, overcoated, booted, string-bag carrying cleaners. The last had piled into the back of the unseated van with cries of 'Any more for the Skylark? . . . Move along down the car, if you please! . . . Room for a small one here, nurse – doctor – off to London, eh . . .? That's nice . . .! Nothing like a change but don't reckon this snow'll change – set in till summer but like they say, worse things happen at sea!' Throughout the drive the women chatted on and cast the pair so many sentimental glances and exchanged so many knowing looks with each other, that both had been privately grateful the womens' romantic natures were spared the disillusion of seeing what transpired after their van disappeared down the road to Ash.

Sam carried both overnight bags into the minute booking hall, then stepped aside, ostensibly to study the chalked list of Sundays only trains whilst Caroline bought a return ticket from the porter-cum-gate-keeper attending the booking office, when his only colleague, the station master, was otherwise occupied. Caroline wore her best coat, it was of black and white tartan tweed and she had made it from a car rug in 1943. She had her thick wavy hair down and a scarlet beret perched on the right side of her head, and matching lipstick. Lipstick was forbidden on duty and seeing her sweetly seductive lips so outlined, and lovely hair floating to her shoulders so disturbed Sam that he was trying to avoid looking at her. He too was dressed for London – aside from the greatcoat – and had a brown corduroy cap Caroline had not seen before and that when the van left the yard had evoked a chorus of delayed wolf-whistles and pleasurably coarse speculations from the cleaning ladies.

Sam's delaying tactics were imposed by the conventions of their mutual backgrounds that insisted if Caroline wanted them to travel up together in the 1.05, then 2.10 from Arumchester, she must first give some small sign of this. She had given none. She was treating him, as on-duty, with that particular form of polite friendliness that is based upon indifference and erects an invisible wall between a man and woman far more successfully than bad manners. During the nights they worked together Sam had grown increasingly aware of the wall, and knowing little about young women when not patients, he had automatically accepted Dick Dunlop's oft-repeated version of why the wall was there. Then slowly, reluctantly, as it meant a constant fight between his intelligence and sexual instincts, his initial great sympathy for Caroline's personal loss, had become tinged with impatience. The war was long over and he felt it time she snapped out of it and got the ghost of the poor Yank out of her bloodstream. Dick had never mentioned he'd been a Yank, but Sam was sure of it from Caroline's habit of slipping unwittingly into US Army slang in tight moments. She was so good in tight moments, that his impatience made him guilty, and consequently, as guilt is not an ennobling emotion, he was often more abrupt to her than he realized.

He handed over her holdall and raised his cap. 'Have a good break.'

'And you, thanks.' She smiled politely and felt rather blank. When he had joined her at the gates she had been very surprised by her relief at the prospect of travelling up with him. She had temporarily forgotten how much she had come to dread arriving in London alone, and especially at Waterloo where she had finally said goodbye to her beloved lover. London had held for her so many once glorious now painful associations that she had only been back twice since coming to the Hut. On both former occasions – as now – it had been to stay with her only brother, an ex-Surgeon–Lieutenant RNVR, and at present assistant in a large general practice in southeast London.

Strolling onto the small platform she knew she should have made the first move, and was afforded another shot of surprised relief by the discovery that for once she had not been solely restrained by the secret – and unsuspected by all but Hoadley East – crushing inferiority complex that was the result of her finally facing what she saw as the truth and an ultimate rejection. Time, and her analytical mind, had demolished as rationalizations her earlier self-explanations about his religion, responsibilities to his wife and son, and the practice he had built-up and waiting for his return to Georgia. She still believed he had loved her deeply in his own way, but distance had convinced her that had not been her way, and that had their positions been reversed, she could never have abandoned him. But just now, she reflected in surprised relief, she had been seeing Sam's angle, not just her's. He was obviously off on a frolic of his own upon which she had no intention of intruding. She could look in a mirror and knew enough of human nature to guess the immediate reaction of any girlfriend waiting for him at Waterloo and seeing them leaving the train together. He rated the break and to live it up on his free Saturday night without her causing an unwanted blot. His girlfriend must live in London or thereabouts, she decided, as if the girl lived down here the grapevine would have caught on. It had only missed out on Jones, partly as she was one of so many and partly as this winter no one could be sure if the yashmak hid a nurse, cleaner, or local resident. But the medical staff were so few, that each was immediately identifiable by his build and walk whatever he wore, and under the spotlight upon any sex when in the acute minority in an enclosed community. She took it for granted he had a girlfriend somewhere outside as this was safest place to have one and that he had a very strong sense of self-preservation was obvious from his coming back from the war. Such inter-staff friendships no longer, as pre-war, put both jobs in jeopardy, but they were not encouraged and unless an engagement was shortly announced, were no help to future careers in Martha's. The announcement was no help to present happiness, being invariably followed by the nurse in question being transferred to another branch. The monastery and the convent still obtain on our hill, she thought, but he's out of the cloisters tonight and I'm not having him wasting good necking time explaining me to her. Dirty trick to make him do so. I'm no threat to any woman. I'm not even one. I'm just an ersatz version all tarted-up for town as that's how the genuine article would be and I'm damned if, on or off-duty, I'm broadcasting that my toothless gums are sucking the bullet.

The third coach seemed the only one empty till she opened the door. Oh, God, no! Mr MacNab!

He was reading a paper in the far, facing window seat. He glanced up as the door opened and leapt smiling to his feet. 'Hallo, Miss Carr! Let's shove that bag aloft for you.'

She smiled politely and thought fast. 'Hallo, Mr MacNab, – thanks!' She spun round as Sam emerged from the booking hall. 'Sam! Lots of room here.'

He had already recognized MacNab in the coach doorway. The situation appealed to his sense of humour. 'Good.' He hurried to join her unsure whether fate was being benevolent or the reverse. They were all standing in the coach when Caroline introduced the men and the train's sudden lurch jolted them off their feet. They fell back laughing on to the two long seats set facing each other. The old armrests were either missing or jammed up, the springs were mostly broken, padding thin, and the seat covers worn and badly stained; the seats' condition was unexceptional in any current British train, as so much rolling-stock had been destroyed in air raids that the country had not yet had the time, steel, or money to replace.

'Rather face, Caro?'

'Fine as we are, thanks, Sam.'

'Good.' She had the window seat, he was beside her and if not close enough to touch, enough to be conscious of her every moment and covertly amused by the sight of MacNab sliding up to the opposite window seat and trying not to look like the cat that's just had the canary snitched from his jaws.

MacNab offered cigarettes and apologies for not having known they wanted this train as there was nothing he enjoyed more than ferrying Hut types to and from the liberty boat. 'Both for Waterloo too? Good Show!' He unbuttoned his ex-RNVR, now insignia-less, officers' greatcoat and bowed to Caroline. 'Shorten the journey no end having such delightful company.' She smiled icily. 'How's tricks up the Hut? No more diphtheria or tractors going bump in the night?'

'All clear, thank you, Mr MacNab.'

'Good show! Old Doc Yardley – our Ash MO, Doc – says you've been damned lucky. My respected mama whom I'm off to visit, would say the good are lucky.' Caroline made no response. Sam bowed. MacNab continued cheerfully, 'Up top –' he waved at the brown cardboard egg-box on the rack over his vacated seat, 'eggs for mama. Round dozen today. Our hens are finally getting back on the job. Cold puts 'em right off – can't blame 'em – so last trip up a meagre four.'

Sam, glancing at Caroline studying the lighted end of her cigarette, said presumably his mother lived in London.

'Anchored in a nursing home, poor old sweet.' MacNab paused, looking troubled. 'Damned tough. I wish we could have her at Widdington, but she needs constant attention. Stroke. Too much for my wife.'

'Much.' Again Sam glanced at Caroline's lowered, composed face. 'Needs skilled and heavy nursing.'

'Knew you'd understand. I try to get up weekly, but can't always make it. Old Tom's cast a spanner in the works – but great to see him going from strength to strength in good old Stanley Parker Ward and as my under-stockman has turned up trumps once more mama gets her eggs.'

Caroline dragged her mind from Kilbride, Jones, and her thoughts before opening the door of this damned coach. 'Should you tell us about them Mr MacNab?'

Sam had to resist the temptation to turn up his coat collar and tell her to stop behaving like a priggish schoolgirl because this rather likeable chap had a smooth tongue and wasn't backward in coming forward. With her looks she had to have spent the last ten years repelling boarders and should by now have learnt to do so with tact and charm.

MacNab was unabashed. 'Not to worry, Miss Carr. I'm not selling 'em. That would be ag'in the law. But we farmers are allowed to keep a meagre fraction of the food we produce for our own consumption and if we choose to hand on any of our portion to an ailing parent, that's legal as hell.'

She coloured faintly. 'I'm sorry. I wasn't thinking.'

'Bless you, I saw that. Miles away.' He smiled into her eyes. 'I promise you this, any black marketeer shoving his nose into my farm would be lucky to get away with just having my dogs set on him.' He looked at Sam. 'I had three years in corvettes on the Atlantic run. After the number of good ships carrying food and petrol to this country I saw go to the bottom, if I had my way, I'd string up every black market type I could lay hands on.'

'I'll go along with that.' Sam looked at the naval greatcoat and thought of his elder brother. 'What were your corvettes' names?'

MacNab gave them. 'Which Army?'

'14th.'

'God Almighty's Own Division, eh? Bags of sun.'

'Bags.' But none in mid-Atlantic on the April night in 1943 when his brother's ship had gone down in two minutes and taken with her the entire ship's company. By the time Sam heard the news, his brother had been dead over two years.

The conversation ranged back and forth between the two men. A ball game played by old pros, thought Caroline, so no hitting the ball too hard and out of court. Old names, places, ports, war jokes and war moans exchanged, but no real truths. Any outsider listening would think their war had been one long laugh, but this is the only way they dare play it, as still far too close.

She gazed out of the window as the men talked on and the little train meandered through a petrified white sea with great frozen waves hiding hedges and ditches, isolated farmhouses and cottages turned into toy sugar houses puffing white wood smoke, and here and there a solitary oak, or little cluster of chestnuts and beeches raising blackened, skeleton arms to the parchment sky. Her thoughts meandered with the train; back to Kilbride in the theatre duty-room; back a little further to Jones, perhaps in her present seat, looking appealingly young and blonde and longing for boyfriends and parties and fun like any other girl of her age from whom the war had taken so much when it took away all the young able men. The war was over, but still no chance of those three in the Hut; on-duty, the responsibilities of mature adults; off, treated like immature schoolgirls; 'lights-out' at 11 p.m., 'no more talking, please nurses', late-leave to midnight seldom granted more than once a month and as seldom sought now the Medical School had gone and the wartime innovation of monthly inter-staff dances in the Lecture Room had been ended by the lack of male partners. Who could blame the poor kid for letting the knockout opposite pick her up? Or he, for doing so at her first glimmer of the green light? He could no more help responding to a come-on than he could breathing. And yet, to be fair, that was only one corner of his picture; in the others, loving father, loving son, good employer, and not improbably, loving husband with far too much nous to go beyond a slap-and-tickle with a pretty girl. A dime to a buck he's a faithful husband, she thought carefully, wolves often are; its the quiet, serious types that fall into the serious traps as they're too innocent to see them coming. He – I – didn't. We should have; we were old enough; we just didn't. No excuse. Statement of fact.

The branchline had begun running parallel with the little river that flowed through Arumchester. The city had grown from the fort the Romans had built at the river's narrowest ford, and centuries later the Normans had left the ruins of the fort in the grounds of the great cathedral they had started building shortly after the Conquest. After more centuries the Roman ruins had been finally demolished by a direct hit from a high-explosive bomb in one of the 'Baedeker raids' made upon some of England's loveliest cathedral cities in November and December 1940. The German bombers had missed the exquisite cathedral so narrowly that it remained lapped by massive, flattened, open spaces that tightened Caroline's throat and hardened the mens' faces. And in unconscious unison they looked thankfully at the ugly, regimented grey lines of pre-fabricated bungalows newly edging long-destroyed streets that in other places were strung with ropes suspending notice-boards announcing that Messrs This and That were open for business at the temporary address below until the new shops could be built on the old sites.

Nice healthy signs and symptoms of Arumchester's reborn phoenix syndrome, reflected Sam, taking from the 'pre-fabs' the comfort he needed more than he knew. He was an exceptionally able young physician, but he was still a young man who had spent most of his life in all-male establishments and long before he left public school been indoctrinated in the belief that the main object of any pretty woman was to please men.

MacNab said thoughtfully, 'Blitzing Arumchester seems so pointless from here. Not that it was. Point of exercise, start up civvy panic, and might have worked if being blitzed in our own backyards didn't make our lot more bloody-minded with rage than fear. Not saying, no fear. I should know. Been yellow as a Jap more times than I've had pink gins. Haven't you, Doc?'

'You have to ask?' retorted Sam evoking the only communal laugh of their journey.

The London train was so crowded that only Caroline had a seat. The men squeezed into the packed corridor just outside her carriage's inner door. She was sorry they had to stand, but now relieved to be on her own and that the old wartime friendliness amongst strangers in trains had been replaced by the far older English custom of treating strange travelling companions as invisible. She had sensed Sam's disapproval of her silence and been belatedly grateful that MacNab's presence diverted Sam's attention, and decided that on balance she had done him a good turn. Being an Englishman he was bound to prefer talking to one of his own sex rather than any woman – and when the three of them left the train at Waterloo, if his girlfriend was waiting, Sam would have no difficulty in writing her, Caroline, off as one of MacNab's popsies.

The train was now in the outskirts of Greater London and with every mile the scars were greater. On either side, in all directions, miles of charred, roofless buildings, mounds of uncleared rubble, huge gaps, some flattened bombsites white sheets of snow and others growing regimented rows of angular grey mushrooms with frozen washing on the lines strung between and narrow front paths and tiny front gardens neatly cleared of snow. The widespread devastation provoked a sudden hum of conversation; immediate post-war memories of the Ruhr, Hamburg, Dresden, Berlin and other German cities were recalled with grim satisfaction by the several young to middle-aged men in demob suits under varying ex-service greatcoats that owned the dark brown trilby demob hats on the racks that were identical with those currently adorning roughly every other male head in the UK. 'Jerry started it. He handed it out. Can't complain that he got it back, can he?'

A worn-faced middle-aged woman in shabby civilian clothes, said tentatively, 'Don't you think it's time we forgot all that?'

'You do that, lady. But don't you try telling it to my old mum and my missus. Bombed out the four times, they were.' The speaker was a youngish man in an ex-airman's greatcoat. Suddenly, he grinned. 'I should worry. Back to my old job in the building trade, I am.' He wagged his head at a window. 'Order books full for years, the guv'nor reckons.'

The coach smiled. Just went to show what was bad for some was good for others. Caroline smiled with her lips. The train was stopping at Waterloo.

That woman was right, thought Caroline about ten minutes later in the rather dim and very cold station 'Ladies'. She studied her freshly touched-up reflection in one of the few extant mirrors and was grateful her eyelashes were dark enough to do without mascara. She was as grateful to Sam's efficacy in first getting rid of MacNab, and after discovering she wanted the Underground, removing himself to the long taxis' queue. He had not asked her destination nor mentioned his own, and from the way he had not taken even one cursory look around the station, he had not expected to be met. So I was wrong there, she thought, but not that woman. I've got to get the hell out of this station! And then she thought, like hell I've got to! Adrian said four at the earliest. Masses of time for a hot cuppa and I am so cold. . . .

She turned up her coat collar, re-adjusted her beret, straightened her back and shot down the stone steps from the cloakroom and across the station into the buffet gazing straight ahead until her eyes met those of Sam who was sitting at a small table against the portion of the far wall that directly faced the entrance. For a second or so they looked at each other and then exchanged the smiles of poker players amused by having their bluff called.

He stood up slowly and she joined him slowly. 'Cold driven you in too, Caro?'

'Yes. Bit warmer in here, thank heaven. I couldn't face one Tube and two trams without a cuppa. How's the coffee?'

'Drinkable. I'll get it. Without, isn't it? How about something to eat?'

'Just coffee, thanks.' She opened her handbag. 'I don't want to offend you, but –'

'Then give it away. I'm the old-fashioned type. Oh –' he misread her expression, ' "give it away" – "let it go" in Australian.'

She knew that. She had met several Australian sisters in the QA that had been caught in England by the war and joined the British Army when their training ended. She didn't say so. She made the conventional reply, and sat down at his empty table thinking how she had never before heard him use Australian slang. She knew why he had been in Australia and had not needed Hoadley's warning to avoid with Sam all references to his captivity and its immediate aftermath. She wondered uneasily what present associations had recalled others to account for the verbal slip, and was suddenly acutely ashamed of the self-preoccupation that, it seemed to her, had given her tunnel-vision in every waking second of her off-duty since last July.

She looked over the table top as if playing pelmanism, noting the half-empty thick white Utility coffee cup, the teaspoonless saucer, the two stubbed out cigarettes in the tin ashtray, the two large sugarless buns yellowed by powdered eggs and the crumbs of the third on a side-plate and the thin, tabloid, latest edition of an evening paper between plate and ashtray. Smoking, eating and reading simultaneously; a 'still life' labelled 'time to kill'. Why? Even if he had no date till later, Martha's was just round the corner – but he had been away five years. Few if any old faces left and probably even fewer he wanted to meet again and face the inevitable 'Long time no see! Where did you get to?' He probably had friends living in London, but with rations and heating tight, few were likely to welcome overnight guests when not members of their own families. Prolonged rationing and prolonged pain had one thing in common; neither brought out the best in human nature. But as the only hope for any resident in any British general hospital off-duty to stay free was to get right away, he had come away and being, Hoadley said, well-heeled, was probably staying at some club. And had time to kill – QED.

He was back. 'Handy you don't take sugar as there's none, and the only teaspoon's chained.'

'Who knows? One day teaspoons may come back.'

'One day,' he agreed, sitting down and noticing every male head had turned in their direction and the envious glances he was collecting. It was so long since he had escorted a desirable woman that he had forgotten the exhilaration it provided. He savoured it sparingly, not letting it go to his head, nor questioning this new turn of fate.

They talked a little of MacNab, and then she told him a little of why she had time in hand and her brother's job and how he lodged with his principal who let her use one of his spare bedrooms whenever she was now in London. 'Very big of him and his housekeeper. Godsend for Adrian. Digs are so short he'd have had a hideous bind finding any near enough. But as the old man says, masses of room in his house now all his children are married and moved out. His wife died sometime in the '30s, his old partner just before the war and he's kept going single-handed till he took on Addie. He was jolly lucky to get the job. Only an assistant as he can't afford to buy into the practice – though what happens when Nye Bevan moves in, neither he nor the principal seem to know.'

'Very prevalent syndrome. Your brother's not married, I take it?'

'Engaged. He was before he applied, but if he hadn't been, he wouldn't have got the job. The old man says his patients don't like unattached doctors and most husbands won't let 'em attend their wives. What really clinched it for Addie is that Jean, his financée's father, is a Benedict's pundit and the principal's a Benedict's man like Addie. So was our father.' She voiced his unspoken question. 'Why am I a Martha? Because my grandmother insisted Martha's only train nice gels and from certain things Daddy let out when he was a student, Benedict's nurses tended to be a little fast, darling.' He grinned. 'Granny goes along with the GBP (Great British Public); only two types of nurses; the sinners and the saints. She's convinced haloes are issued with all Martha's caps and I had to have her consent to train as I was still a minor, and she'd become my legal guardian. She's been marvellous to Addie and me since our mother died. 1930. Leukaemia.'

His dark eyes filled with compassion. 'Tough. I'm sorry.'

'Thanks. Yes, it was.' And recognizing that particular compassion, she added, 'Your parents too?' He nodded and they exchanged their first empathetic glance of that afternoon. She looked away first and down at the ungainly china on the stained cracked yellow oilcloth table cover and then at the shabby figures in the ubiquitous mixture of old civvy and service clothes patiently queuing at the counter or sitting at the other tables. 'Sometimes, I'm almost grateful for their sakes that my parents aren't around now. They were both so sure there'd never be another war after their "war to end war" and that the British Empire was fixed as tomorrow's sunrise – hurt them too much.' There was a warmth in her husky voice he had only previously heard her use to patients. 'This cold new world of rations and nothing working properly wouldn't have figured to them.' She looked at him. 'Daddy was in the RAMC last time round. France, Dardanelles, Salonika. He died in '38 just after Munich. Pneumonia. No penicillin or sulphas then, just prontosil. Didn't touch him.'

'In Benedict's?'

She shook her head. 'Home. He was a pathologist on hols. We had in a day and a night nurse, and one was a Martha.' She smiled faintly. 'In retrospect she was probably why I let

Granny twist my arm – not that I had much hope.' Her face was suddenly alight with affectionate laughter. 'At arm-twisting, my grandmother rides point. During the war she used it to run her local WVS and now she's at it with the Parochial Church Council, her bridge club and, for the last couple of weeks, boosting anti-dip jabs around rural Devon.'

'Good for her.' He had to pause to collect his thoughts as she was looking as different from the girl she had been on the way up – and the Night Office – as one of those pictures in the painting books he had had as a child, after the black and white drawing was washed with a paint-brush dipped in water that brought out the colours. 'Incidentally, you're due a pat on the back here. On the run from Arumchester MacNab said he'd taken your advice and has managed to persuade his wife to let the school doctor immunize their elder sons and have the baby done once he's a year old. Too bad we can't turn you and your grandmother loose on the GBP.'

'I'm glad that's taken care of,' she said with an icy note that now puzzled rather than irritated him. 'But needs more than Granny and I to put this over at large, Sam.'

'Too bloody right.' He stubbed out his cigarette with un-necessary force. 'This specific national ostrich syndrome drives me up the wall. Our MOH told me he's been beating his head against it, years. He wasn't around when it hit Ash in '33, but as he kept saying, he would have thought local legend would have done the trick of getting it over that dip's no Act of God, but a preventable disease with a disgracefully high annual death-rate. High and unnecessary.' His eyes blazed with concerned anger. 'Hasn't got through.' He looked round the buffet. 'Like London. And as the bug's always endemic this time of the year, odds-on that within shouting distance there's either a "carrier" or someone cooking dip. GBP just couldn't care less.' He looked back at her. 'Don't ask me why. I just wish to God I knew.'

She looked at him blankly for the few seconds it took her professional mind to overcome conventions and her inferiority complex. 'If you're not doing anything special for the next couple of hours, come and meet Addie. Might help you on this one. But – er – if you can't spare the time – just sound off.'

5

'No sense your pushing that bell, miss! Not no one home. If you're wanting the doctor you'd best go on in and wait for him.'

The raucous female voice came from just behind them on the cracked pavement of a side street on the river side of the local High Street. The side street was lined with lower-middle class Edwardian terraced houses and they were on the door-step of the one that contained the secondary and oldest surgery that for Caroline's present purpose was a more convenient meeting point than the principal's house as this was over a mile from the nearest tram or bus stop.

They turned to the speaker, an elderly woman so layered with wraps that she was broad as short. She had one hand on the handle of a massive old pram containing a sleeping baby and the other gripping the reins of toddler similarly wrapped with only eyes, pink nose and red cheeks visible. The woman peered up at Caroline and let out an amiable shriek. 'I knows you, miss! You knows me! It's Mrs Donkin as caretakes for the doctors and you'll be Miss Carr and can't be no other, seeing you're the dead spit of the Young Doctor and I minds his fetching you round afore Christmas! Not as you'd know me for all I got on but in this cold do you wonder? But you and your gentleman'll be wanting to get in out of it,' she went on returning Caroline's apologetic smile with a toothless beam and allowing no other interruption. 'The Young Doctor's not come in from his morning calls – on the late side, he is, but would be, wouldn't he, seeing its the Old Doctor's free Saturday – will you leave off, Bette, lovey!' She beamed on the now struggling toddler. 'Trying to fetch off your old nan's arm same as your Uncle Bertie's are you? You go in, miss! Not locked – well, wouldn't be right, would it, seeing its the surgery and if I sees the Young Doctor whiles I'm up the shops I'll say as you're waiting with your gentleman friend and you'll pardon me not stopping but I just stepped in for the word with my neighbour Mrs Hargreaves and her daughter-in-law come in to say as Black, the butcher's up our side the High Street got in some mince off-ration. Horsemeat, I'll be bound, but don't do to ask, do it? And what I says is I hope the horse had a happy life and we all got to go. Isn't that so, sir?'

Sam, outwardly decorously and inwardly joyously, lifted his cap. He had attended innumerable Mrs Donkins in pre-mid-'41 Martha's. 'It is Mrs Donkin.'

Caroline said, 'Thank you, Mrs Donkin. Nice to see you again. You and the family keeping well?'

'Nicely, ta, miss. Anytime, miss. Just stand in the hall and shout up,' she added cryptically, to Sam, 'TTFN.' She moved off hitching the reins to the handle and informing the suddenly wailing Bette that she was asking for the back of her old nan's hand and needn't think she'd not get it just as the Young Doctor's young lady sister and her gentleman friend was having the butcher's. The wails promptly stopped and the toddler danced alongside the pram.

'Better get in.' Caroline sounded and felt uncertain. She had begun regretting her impulsive invitation before they left Waterloo, as though her common sense insisted Sam had enough of the same to take it as professionally evoked, she still needed the armour of her uniform to be sure of her ground. She had to remind herself sharply to stop being neurotic before she could turn the knob in her gloved hand.

Sam registered her uncertainty and that the front door, as

all in that street and area of London, was so engrimed and charred that the original colour of the peeling paintwork was undetectable. That house, as most, had new glass in the windows, but omnipresent were the filthy strips of old anti-blast paper stuck to the sills, and stonework badly chipped, cracked and charred by old air raids.

The front door opened into a dim slit of a hall blocked on one side by the narrow, uncarpetted, wooden staircase running up to a tiny landing. On the other side were two doors; the first was marked PATIENTS' WAITING ROOM, PLEASE WALK IN, in faded black capitals, the second SURGERY, PLEASE DO NOT ENTER BY THIS DOOR, in faded red. Sam noticed stairs and doors, second. His first attention was gripped by a smell that he might have forgotten from his three weeks as a district midwifery clerk in early 1938, but could never forget for later reasons.

Caroline glancing at his rigid face in the dim light, said unhappily, 'Yes. Bugs. Plus cockroaches and fleas. Addie and his boss have tried everything. Nothing shifts 'em. The boss says too embedded in the structure and the only solution is to burn the place down and the only reason why he's sorry Jerry didn't do that job is that it would have left Mrs Donkin homeless.' She gestured up the stairs. 'She's lived and raised no one's clear how many generations of her family up there since before the Great War. She used to pay five bob a week,' she continued plugging Mrs Donkin as it was relaxing some of his rigidity, 'and get two bob back for keeping the place clean and letting in those patients that don't just walk in, up to the General Strike (1926). I don't know just how much her pay then went up, but she now gets twenty-five shillings a week, and though the boss is happy for her to pay no rent she insists on giving him two bob weekly as quote, never had no charity, ta, doctor, and not wishing to start, unquote.'

His lips smiled. 'Good on her.'

'Yes.' She turned away and with her back to him, said, 'I'm feeling a heel, Sam. I should've realized that –'

'Shoving the silver spoon down my throat might choke me.

Worth it, for what you think and I suspect'll turn out to be a dead handy bit of professional insight.' He opened the waiting-room door for her. 'If I choke, thump me on the back.' The grubby net curtains on the front windows made the room nearly as dim as the hall. His hand felt for a light switch before he realized none existed. 'All right if I light one of these gas lamps, Caro?'

'Hold it, till I've put a bob in the meter to be sure.' She ducked behind one of the hard chairs lining the walls and fed in a shilling. 'Okay. Thanks. Much better.' She looked at the small, ancient gas fire that was protected by a heavy iron fireguard that must have come from a Victorian nursery. 'We'll leave that and light the one in the surgery. Thisaway.' She opened a connecting inner door.

Sam did a quick survey of the hard chairs, the low, old bamboo table neatly stacked with tin-lid ashtrays, tattered copies of old magazines and childrens' comics, the rocking horse and doll's house in one corner that looked of the same provenance as the fireguard, the threadbare marble-patterned fawn and brown linoleum on the floor, the row of old green baize boards on the walls bearing notices advising patients of surgery hours, telephone numbers, where to leave messages when the surgery was empty and to PLEASE ALWAYS WRITE YOUR NAMES, ADDRESSES AND AGES IN CAPITAL LETTERS LIKE THIS.

There was no mention of the patients' telephone numbers since none using that waiting room had private telephones. And he noticed something more in the soft glow of the gas-lighting, and that was the atmosphere in the cold empty room that almost erased the associations with the smell clinging to the back of his throat. Comforting he thought, following Caroline into the surgery where she had lit one gas lamp and was stooping to light the fire.

'The principal's wanted to close this surgery for years.' She dropped the used match into an ashtray on a smallish zinc-topped kitchen table against the window wall and on the far side of the deep stone sink that had a miniature gas geyser fitted to the piping above its single tap. On the zinc table was a gas-ring and beside it, a large fishkettle, and old two-pint jam jar filled with disinfectant holding two pairs of long-handled forceps. 'The patients won't wear it. Most much prefer this to his bigger and better surgery up at the house and that,' she nodded towards the inner door he had just closed, 'to using his dining-room as a waiting room. Also, this place is far easier for most being so near the High Street and they've always used it. If you want to smoke, its okay. All ether, meths and other inflammables, in here.' She moved to what he had taken for the door of a cupboard in the corner of the outer wall about one yard behind the desk and took down a large key from the top lintel. 'This used to be the old scullery when this was a kitchen. The boss's predecessor had it gutted and all this put in.' She unlocked the door. 'Take a look.'

'All this' were the deep shelves stacked with ranks of bottles that lined the long narrow room that at the far end had another stone sink under a window. The sink had zinced draining boards on both sides; on one was another gas-ring and fishkettle; on the other in neat order, a pair of apothecaries' scales and measuring equipment and a row of mortars and pestles. On the top shelves on both sides were ranks of clean, empty, medicine bottles and two former confectioners' glass jars crammed with new corks. 'They do most of their own dispensing in here. Obviously, anything complex they get from chemists. They, not the patients. The patients using this surgery don't like the chemist. They like leaving with the bottle in their hands.'

'Like in Cas. in London.' He moved to peer at the labels on the rows of bottles filled with 'stock' medicines, tablets and lotions. 'Where do they keep their DDs? (Dangerous Drugs).'

'In the locked cupboard inside the second deal cupboard in there,' she jerked her head at the surgery, 'and their medical bags.' He had taken up a huge bottle of cochineal and was holding it up to the light. 'Their patients like pink medicines and pink pills. They believe they work better, hence all those pink aspirin. The boss says as that's what they believe, it does work better.'

'Sounds a good psychologist.'

'He is. He's a marvellous GP, Addie says and can make a diagnosis from the way a patient walks in from the waiting room. He growls and grunts like Hoadley and the patients love him.'

'Like Hoadley.'

'Yes.' They exchanged smiles as he came out, relocked the door and replaced the key. 'When I was last here the old boy told me when he was a Benedict's houseman at the turn of this century they were still using Lister's carbolic spray and stringing carbolic-soaked sheets round their theatres.'

'Like Ferdie. Just one generation on from surgeons operating in frock coats stiff with dried blood and patients' developing "laudable pus". Nothing to beat world wars for speeding up medical advances.' He looked from the one hard chair on one side of the hearth to the other facing the doctor's at the desk. The doctor's chair also faced the inner door and the old black rexine, horsehair-stuffed examination couch against the opposite inner wall. 'Will your brother be offended if I shift his chair to the fire for you?'

She shook her head. 'He's always doing it. Thanks.' She put the desk ashtray on the hearth between them. 'Sorry he's taking so long.'

'I'm in no hurry. If the poor chap hasn't yet had lunch he's the one that needs your sympathy.'

She sat down. 'Saturday's lunch is never before teatime as there's only one on. Weekdays Addie thinks he's done well to have lunch by half-two.'

'Roughly, how many house-calls?'

'Between thirty and forty daily. Three surgeries on weekdays. Nine-to-ten mornings up at the house only; evenings, seven-to-eight at the house, six-to-eight, here. Saturdays, usual morning one at the house, only evening one, seven-to-eight, here. No surgeries Sundays, just calls. They share all day and night calls and box-and-cox the surgeries, and the boss is good about taking all night calls on the two nights after Addie's weekly half-day and alternate Saturday.

Sundays they settle according to calls, but one is always, on-call.'

He was very interested. He had heard and read much of this in pre-his-war Martha's and the Hut, but as he now appreciated, always with the detachment of a hospital doctor too preoccupied by his own great hospital to have the time or inclination for serious consideration of what lay beyond its walls. 'Mind my asking what he gets?'

'Good money for an MB, BCh. Twenty a month, all found. Same as Hoadley. What do you?'

'Fifteen.' He didn't add that his small private income reduced his monthly pay cheque to £4 after tax. 'How many patients in this practice?'

She had to think. And watching her absorbed face in the soft amberish light, and listening to the soft hiss of the gas, he again sensed the comforting atmosphere in that impoverished little surgery that must have witnessed so much suffering, fear, anxiety and grief but had for the patients waiting in the next room the inestimable comfort of knowing the other side of the door, with no starch, no red tape in between, was the doctor they had come to see and, where the principal was concerned, had probably known, if only by sight, all their lives.

Caroline said, 'Hard to say as though I think they've got about eighteen hundred Panel patients, this is a Half-Crown practice. My guess is, three to four thousand. As I've told you, covers a huge area.'

'All non-Panel patients have to fork out?'

'Yes. But what they fork varies with what they get. It's two shillings-and-sixpence to visit the surgery, but that covers the medicine, pills, lotion or whatever. Two bob, without. Three-and-six for a house-call, and whatever, cash down.' She stared into the fire. 'The cash side upset Addie badly when he started. In Benedict's, like Martha's, hard cash is neither mentioned nor thought of. He says at every visit, the sad little heap of pennies and sixpences are always waiting by the front door and shoved at him before he sees the patient. In here –' she looked at him 'the non-Panels walk in holding out the half-crown or two bob. The poor don't run up bad debts with the doctor.' She smiled ironically. 'That's the middle and upper classes' prerogative.'

He knew what was coming and forestalled it.

'I've heard Ferdie on that one. Half-crown for an anti-dip?'

Her smile vanished. 'Officially, here. The boss often tries to waive the fee, but his patients go along with Mrs Donkin on charity. Pride matters, especially when you've so little of anything else and Sam – millions have so little.' Her voice suddenly vibrated with anger and she had to stop to control it. Then she said, 'A half-crown mayn't sound much, unless all you've got to keep the entire family is two to three pounds a week – and that's a good wage round here – or, if you're a war-widow with young children, with luck, twenty to thirty shillings. Most get less. Ten bob a week for the childless, like Old Age Pensioners. So laying out the extra cash purely as a prevention against something little Joan or Johnny might not get or might get and get over like young Mabel, Tom, or Mrs Whatsit upstairs or down the basement, isn't the first thing you think of when the rent man won't wait, the grocer won't put more on the slate, the eldest child's grown out of its shoes, and there's only a few bob left to feed the family till next pay or pension day. Pay-day's Friday round here. Addie's been horrified by the discovery that the most usual Thursday's high tea is bread-and-scrape.' She fell silent for a few moments then looked straight into his concerned face. 'Yes. It is 1947 and yes, we did win the war.' He could only shake his head. 'Of course, another reason for the apparent "couldn't care less" is that dip's so common. Everyone round here's met it again and again – like the old bombs. They had to get used to both dangers, and one of the worst things about poverty and war is the way both teach you to get used to things that no one should accept.'

'That's for sure. Everything you've said is for sure. I should've worked it out as –'

'You had other things on your mind. Like Addie. Tell you something else –' but she broke off.

'Go on. Please.'

'Well – and hold on to your adrenalin – but when Addie came here he was as vehemently anti-National Health Service as every Martha's man with whom I've discussed it. Just mention Nye Bevan to Hoadley and he blows all fuses. But Addie's now as vehemently pro as I've been since I heard of it.'

He said evenly, 'My adrenalin's in good shape. You and me, both. What converted you?'

She stared ignoring the query. 'You? Pro? You've never said in the Hut.'

'Old hand at keeping my head down.'

She smiled wonderfully. 'Until you decide to stick your neck out – hold it –' but he was on his feet at the sound of doors opening. Then almost immediately a man's voice shouted. 'I can't wait, doctor!' The inner door was flung open and a figure in a RAF balaclava and greatcoat all but fell through. 'The doctor's old Baby (Austin) ain't outside but I seen the lights – he must be here!' He hauled back the woollen helmet from his sweating face and glared at Sam. 'You ain't Dr Carr and if you and your good lady's got him you got to step aside. I got to fetch him out! Where's he gone? In with the bottles?'

Caroline had risen. She said quickly, 'I'm afraid Dr Carr's not back yet but he shouldn't –'

'I got to have him, miss! I just run from the house and the woman said the Old Doctor's off Chatham for the day and Dr Carr's on and always steps in here to pick up messages before going back for his dinner and gives her the tinkle from here and no sense her trying to ring here as he'd not rung her yet and wouldn't be none to answer.' He glared at the old-fashioned, upstanding black telephone with a trumpet earpiece on the desk. 'I just met old Ma Donkin up the street and she says he not got back when she come out and I'd catch him here and I got to! I got to have him! The wife's took bad – real bad. Standing talking normal the one minute, she was, and next she was down on the kitchen floor – couldn't say nothing – couldn't seem to breathe – couldn't do nothing but look at me and gone white as a sheet.' His sharp face unconsciously mimicked the dreadful fixed stare of great pain. 'Just looked, see – so I shouted for me neighbour and she come quick and I carries the wife on to our bed and left her with me neighbour to fetch the doctor.' He only then took in the situation. 'Not back from his calls?' He flopped on to the edge of the examination couch. 'I can't go back without him. Hurting her cruel, I could tell – I got to help her – but I got to have the doctor – I promised her I'd fetch him quick – I got to have him! If I just waits – I dunno what'll not –' He was too distressed to finish the sentence.

Caroline looked at Sam and knew what was coming before his barely perceptible nod. He turned to the man. 'What's your name, please?'

'Baker, sir. The wife – she's Mrs Rita Baker, age 44 and I got –' He fumbled for a scrap of paper with the essential details in hastily pencilled capitals, and hope leapt into his distraught face. 'Reckon you can reach the doctor, sir?'

'I'm afraid not, Mr Baker.' Sam took the scrap, glanced at it, then handed it to Caroline. 'Listen, Mr Baker. I'm a friend of Miss Carr's waiting with her for her brother and I am not a general practitioner. But I am a doctor of medicine. My name is Dr Browne, and if you wish I'll come back to your wife with you and Miss Carr will wait here and bring on Dr Carr directly he arrives. I'm afraid I've no car. If we can't find a taxi, tram any use? Or quicker to walk?'

'Tidy walk, but – oh, ta, sir! Yea, ta –' The man leapt from the couch. 'Oh, thank Gawd – yea – I'd be ever so obliged, doctor, and I got,' he dug into a pocket and held out a small handful of change, 'three-and-a-tanner.'

'Put that away until you see Dr Carr, Mr Baker.' Sam spoke gently but the order was unmistakeable. 'I'll just get my – oh thanks, Miss Carr.' She had handed him his overnight bag that, as she had guessed, contained the basic essentials for the commonest medical emergencies and without which no medically qualified doctor of her acquaintance ever travelled on even the shortest journey.

A minute later she was alone. She glanced at her watch, then dated and timed in the waiting open exercise book Mr Baker's arrival and message, but did not add the details of his departure. Talk that over with Addie first, she thought, returning to her chair by the fire and smoothing out the scrap of paper in her hands. From Baker's verbal description and that look on his face, it was a classic coronary and as his wife had been alive when he left her, probably not too big and with speedy treatment might pull through. But any size coronary was a terrifying experience for the patient and any onlookers, especially if close relatives. Mrs Baker needed morphia and oxygen stat. Sam would give her the first, and knowing him, unless Addie showed up fast get her to the second, fast. Martha's? No, Benedict's was nearer and, as all the voluntary hospitals, would take without notice anything from a coronary to a splinter in a finger. All that was necessary, day or night, was for the patient to arrive in Casualty. Splinters had to wait for attention; coronaries jumped all queues. He'll send Baker to find a taxi rather than waste more time trying to find a public phone box and call an ambulance. Addie says so many public boxes are still down from the war that finding one in service takes ages. Baker'll tell Sam, she decided, and that far more hope of grabbing a taxi in the High Street. The shot'll stop the pain and help shock, and being carried on to the back seat of a taxi with Sam to keep her steady and her husband to hold her hand, will be far less strain for her than the inevitable, agonizing wait for the ambulance.

She looked again at her watch. Gone twenty minutes. If Addie didn't show up in the next few, Sam would go into action and then, after, he'd deal with the little matters like established medical ethics and Martha's iron rule that no residents treat any patients outside the hospital. This could easily cost him his job – and had he decided to do Sweet Fanny Adams, as easily cost Mrs Baker her life. So how in hell can I wish to God I hadn't brought him here this afternoon? Talk about the luck of the draw for Mrs Baker – or didn't luck really come into it?

Her mind began re-tracing the thread to MacNab, to Pat Jones, to the dip outbreak, and there the thread bifurcated and she followed the separate threads to her own and Sam's pasts that had severally made them the people they were in the present and so, for differing reasons, when free this afternoon, with time to kill. She was still turning this conclusion over when, some twenty minutes later, her brother rushed in wearily. He had just stopped his Austin in the High Street to buy cigarettes, been hailed from the long queue outside the butchers by Mrs Donkin, and driven straight on.

'Sorry you've had to hang around, Caro.' He pushed back his trilby and stooped to kiss her cheek. 'My last three calls were miles off and the last one took ages. How much chicken-pox have you seen and got any fags? I'm out and I've got a problematical case. The kid's pustules are coming out first on the extremities and her face, like smallpox, but even if she hadn't been vaccinated, she doesn't look like a smallpox. Not ill enough.'

Adrian Carr was nearly as tall and twice as solid as Sam. She gave and lighted the cigarette for him first, then rested her hands on the shoulders of his old naval greatcoat from which his fiancée had removed the insignia. 'Sorry, honey, haven't seen chickenpox in years and I'm afraid you've more than that problematical case.' She showed him the scrap of paper.

6

'Bright chap, your brother. Just the job, this joint.' Sam gave her another of his polite little smiles across their candlelit, red-and-white check-clothed, restaurant table, then looked round. 'I'm glad my tie's anonymous.'

'I too have this allergy to being lynched,' she said and they both laughed almost naturally.

The restaurant, still in its wartime basement, was in one of the side streets just behind St Benedict's Hospital that for the last century had been Martha's traditional rival on the opposite bank of the Thames. From the appearances and overheard snatches of hospital 'shop', ninety per cent of their fellow diners were from Benedicts and the majority, couples a few years younger than themselves, in free-Saturday-night mood. A short while back when this power cut started it was greeted with joyous cheers and cries of 'Thank God we're off!' The diners had lighted their own candles before the waiters could produce matches or the pianist put one to the hurricane lamp on the lid of his piano. The band, a quintet, was taking a break, mopping brows, downing half-pints, and the euphoria in the smoke-hazed atmosphere that was always present at hospital staff parties was reminding Caroline of Sister Preliminary Training School's long-forgotten 'You will discover, nurses, that none enjoy their off-duty like young nurses and young doctors since both professions have so little free time.' And the operative word there, thought Caroline, is 'young'. On paper we're not much older; in reality, a good twenty years.

'More of whatever this is Caro?'

'Turnips or parsnips, I'm not sure which. It's very nice, only no more, thanks. I'm doing fine,' she insisted with such sincerity that he nearly believed her. They had decided on grilled whalesteak as their main course rather than the only other choice, 'Snoek à la mode'. She was doing her best to conceal her struggle to swallow the meat and it was a good best, as to dissemble to her host in particular and men in general upon social occasions had been instilled from her early childhood first by her Edwardian mother and then Victorian grandmother, both of whom would have been not merely impatient but appalled by her behaviour to MacNab this afternoon . . . this is a man's world, darling, and women must remember it . . . She had never questioned nor disobeyed their maxims until, in Normandy mud, she began thinking for herself and a few months later living if only inwardly, by her own rules. But when it suited her, as now, she played by the old, as these provided the stronger armour. 'Won't you finish up the whatever, Sam?'

'No thanks. Had enough.' His mind was elsewhere, so for once he no longer marvelled at that statement. 'Haven't you of that whale? Let it RIP.'

'If you don't mind, I will.' She looked down at her plate, partially as his perception was disturbing and partially from . . . at a dinner-table, darling, when not conversing in turn with the gentlemen on her left and right, a lady should keep her eyes downcast. . . .

'I'm sorry we didn't go for the snoek.'

The genuine concern in his voice made her look up. He was playing by the old rules and so well that he was surprising her by showing the same consideration for her comfort that she had grown accustomed to from an American Southerner but ceased to expect from an Englishman of her wartime generation, if only, she belatedly recalled, as this was her first date with one since Hoadley in 1945.

She smiled properly. 'Heaven forbid! How I wish Dr Edith had left that poor fish swimming happily round the Indian Ocean or wherever instead of bunging it into tins to boost Britain's protein. Smells fishy, looks fishy and tastes foully fishy no matter how disguised. At least if you drown whale in enough onions, like this, you almost drown the taste. Can you remember roast beef? I can't?' She heard herself and stiffened in self-reproach at that thoughtless intrusion upon his forbidden territory.

'Can I? Oh my word, sport, too bloody right I can!' He electrified her by switching into broad Australian. 'If you want a good hunk of the bloody roast, sport, you can't beat bloody Sydney. As for the T-bones they dish out in midnight picnics on Bondi Beach – bloody beauts! Sorry about the bloodies,' he added in his own voice, 'Australian term of endearment.'

She laughed properly and stifling the urge to stand up and cheer him, lied, 'I had forgotten your sojourn in the Antipodes, Ghastly comedown coming back to this lot. Comedown for us all.' She spread her hands. 'There we all were having won the war and expecting to come back to days of wine and roses, and what did we get? Days of whalemeat and snoek. Don't say it, Sam!'

He was laughing properly. 'What?'

'I'll wear it.'

Their laughing eyes exchanged a glance that neither had previously shared with the other, then looked quickly away. That time Sam studied his empty plate. He was finding her sudden change of mood as disorientating as her appearance tonight. She had changed from the sweaters and skirt she had worn earlier into the one dress she had brought to wear tomorrow when lunching with Adrian and his future in-laws – the basic reason for her visit. She had made the black corduroy dress since coming to the Hut, with an open shirt collar, three-quarter sleeves, fitted belted waist and far fuller flared skirt than the law allowed Utility ready-made dresses or skirts. She had chosen corduroy as it was only five shillings and two coupons a yard against the more expensive and five to six

94

needed for other winter dress material, and black, as it suited her and she had needed every morale booster she could lay hands on. The darkness and soft lines heightened the beauty of her pale skin, the gentle curves of her tall, slender figure, and, to Sam, her femininity and an elusive quality of sophistication that he had never previously noticed and was collecting for him even more envious male glances than in the buffet this afternoon. He would have been astonished and incredulous had he suspected that whilst he was studying his plate Caroline was belatedly noticing she was collecting the same from more than a few girls at the neighbouring tables. She looked at him more closely and saw how the candlelight by youthening his face made him quite strikingly good-looking and how the greying streaks added the touch of distinction. Then she remembered something Addie had passed on to her this afternoon and thought, not just the candlelight.

'Will no complaints pass the censor?'

'I'd say so.'

'So would I.' He had to look back at her.

'What if I have just hocked the silver spoon for our night out on the town at the five statutory bob a head plus three bob cover charge? What if we have just had a soup of unknown and best undiagnosed origins and, to follow the wretched whale, can settle for a dubious trifle or revoltingly deep purple blancmange? What if the wine had run out before we showed up?' He raised his glass that held a third of the half-pint that was now the allowance per customer as the beer was running out. 'This beer once met a hop. Not more than once, but who's narking? Not me. A long time since I last had a night on the tiles.'

It was a long time since she had seen her brother's tired face look so relieved as after the phone call Sam made from a public box in Benedict's just as she was finishing her explanation. 'Apologetic chap.' Addie replaced the ear-piece on the hook. 'He should worry. I need an apology from a man with Membership coping with one of my cardiacs like I need a hole in the head. I take it you heard most. He's bringing his notes to the house.'

She nodded without comment as not only was this consultation essential, but to defer outwardly to her two-years-older brother had also been instilled in her from the nursery. 'No sweat over the boss's reaction. He'll give a good belly laugh, ask when I've ever known him look a gift horse in the mouth and throw in a crack about the uses of a pretty sister.' He helped himself to another of her cigarettes then rang Benedict's and asked by name for the cardiac registrar, who had been in his own student year. 'Adrian Carr here, Mike. Hi! *Re* one Mrs Rita Baker, age 44 – yes? . . . yes . . . yes . . . good . . . he did?' He grinned. 'That so? . . . Membership . . . keeps the books straight . . . What's that? Some other time, old chap. I'll be in touch. Thanks, Mike.' He rehooked the ear-piece. 'She's having the works, on the DIL, hubby *in situ*, and as they got her so quickly Mike thinks there's a fair chance she'll make it. What he wants to know is how I had a medical pundit on temp standby. Chap looked so damned distinguished, Mike said, that he wished he'd had a closer shave this morning. Fill me in on the bits on Browne you've left out, on the way to the house. You can kick off with why you've got him in tow. Switch off that fire. I'll douse the lights.'

She gave him the whole story on the drive and included 'Ex-Jap POW.'

'Poor bastard, but *ipso facto* a tough bastard. No wonder he scared the living daylights out of poor old Mike.' They had reached the house and he glanced at her before switching off the particular inside light he had put in when he bought the 1934 car for £15 last summer. 'Just good friends?'

'No. Professional buddies.'

'Lot of that about. Let's get in. My stomach's flapping against my spinal column.'

When Sam arrived, he and she had tea whilst Adrian finished his lunch, then the men disappeared into the 'new' surgery (it was over forty years old), and the housekeeper followed her usual custom of taking Caroline into the kitchen to reiterate the problems of keeping food warm and palatable for hours. 'In nineteen years, Miss Carr, not the once have I been able to serve a meal on time. . . .'

When Caroline rejoined the men, they were talking chicken-pox and Adrian was saying, 'If you're sure you wouldn't mind?'

'Quite. My time's my own.'

The two men left together shortly to return over an hour later agreeing it was chickenpox and that it wasn't the first time the chaps that wrote the books hadn't come up with all the answers. Then Adrian disappeared to get ready for evening surgery in the 'old' and Sam returned to Caroline in the sitting-room, she assumed to say he was off.

'Your brother's just told me he can get me a table at a rather decent joint near Benedict's. If you'd care to dine with me, I'd like it very much.'

She was hesitant. 'Look, Sam, you've done more than enough. You really don't have to –'

He was abrupt. 'Nor do you. How about it?'

'I – I'd have to change.'

'I'm in no hurry. Yes?'

'Okay – er – thanks.'

Through Adrian they had a table on the edge of the smallish round dance floor. Adrian had once served in the same destroyer as the proprietor and before that known him from his years in Medical School. 'Booked solid, doc – not to panic – I'll bung in the extra for two. . . .' They had earlier agreed to eat before dancing, but as Sam lowered his beer glass, the pianist began vamping the opening of 'Lazy Bones' and their heads turned to him in identical pleasure.

'Do we wait, Caro? Or may we?'

'Let's.'

She came slowly into his arms and he held her lightly, but closely, as there was no other fashion of dancing a slow foxtrot well and he was a good dancer. So was she and after the first few steps their mutual discovery of this immediately relaxed their instinctive tension at the physical proximity that social conventions still ordained were only permissable to the single on a dance floor. They danced 'Lazy Bones' in an unstrained, silent enjoyment, but as the quintet proved to be in a Hoagy Carmichael medley and slid without pause into 'Small Fry', 'Lazy River', and 'The Nearness of You', their silence developed new strains of its own that for Sam were interwoven with enchantment, and for Caroline with an element that she suspected was guilt but refused to spoil the moment by analysing. She loved dancing with a good partner and she loved this music. When the fourth tune ended, she gave a small sigh that for the instant transported Sam to a secret place of soft darkness and her soft warm body in his arms.

He was still holding her when the trumpeter soloed a shower of notes. She tilted back her head, smiling half-eagerly, half-anxiously, 'This breaks into a jive. Do you?'

He had recognized 'The Old Music Master' and took quick cover in Australia. 'I'd have you know, sport, my jive on Bondi Beach had the wowsers up in arms.' She laughed and he drew her closer and danced on slowly to the sudden change in rhythm. Holding tightly to her hand he swung her out at arms' length and was as delighted by her response as the other couples. The floor exploded into jivers and the band literally played up in the instinctive recognition of jazz musicians to a suddenly vastly appreciative audience, repeating and pro-longing with improvisations the fast intermissions alternating with the slow and the few sitters-out stopped talking and eating to listen and watch. And Caroline, clinging to Sam's hand, jiving and laughing with her hair flying, skirt swirling, watching his laughing face, normally tidy hair falling forward and tie flapping, and the innate grace in his absurd antics, had the sensation of watching from her own shoulder the return to vibrant life and youth the man she and the Hut once labelled 'that poor old wreck L.B.' And in one of those flashes of insight that can illuminate more than hours of intro-spection, she recognized that for these past four months he had still been anaesthetized by the protracted delayed-action shock of his release from the years of nightmare and that, as for any patient coming out of an anaesthetic, there was always the right moment for surfacing to full consciousness, and this was his. She was glad for him, and though this she did not yet properly appreciate, glad for herself, to be here and watching his moment and having such fun. She had forgotten that sometimes life could be just plain fun, as whilst she had known great happiness with her lover, always that happiness had been shadowed by the guilt of the present and dread of the future.

The melody ended as gently as it had opened and to yells, claps and stamps of applause from the tables. The quintet gave boxers' salutes and the jiving couples flopped breathlessly against each other. Caroline, moved her hand from Sam's left shoulder to push back her hair. 'Those wowsers didn't know a good thing when they saw it.'

'Never saw you at it.' He tossed back his head to get his forelock out of his eyes. He couldn't bear to release a hand for the job until he had no alternative. 'Had enough?' But again the solo trumpeter was improvising. 'One more for the road?'

'Sure!' She had spoken before she realized the tune being improvised was 'Georgia on my Mind'. She had never known if the title applied to a girl or the State, but it had only one association for her. And as they danced, with that peculiar ability of past, unrepeatable joy to drive in the knife, it went in deeper with every slow, insidiously sensuous beat of the lovely, lilting melody. Not only deeper, but exposing old reasoned guilt; new unreasoned guilt at having been enjoying herself in another man's arms; long stifled guilt over what her parents, her grandmother would have felt and said, could they have known the truth; what Addie would have said; what Sam would say; what Hoadley had said . . . No sense binding about double-standards, my girl – that's the way the world is, always has been, always will be, as it's women not men that get pregnant – yes, it's bloody tough, but so is life and never more so than for any illegitimate kid whose mother had the education and intelligence to say 'no', but not the guts! You've done gynae. You know the only one hundred per cent certainty of staying out of an ante-natal clinic is to bloody say it. . . .

She had to close her eyes and follow Sam's lead like an automaton. He felt the alteration at once and glancing down saw the desolation in her closed face and guessing some of what was happening had consciously to stifle the suggestion that they change their minds and sit this one out. Not just in the bloodstream, but joined the party, he thought in a bleak disappointment that demolished enchantment. He hoped for both their sakes this power cut would last until this travesty of a dance was over.

It did.

'Thanks very much. That was great.'

She dropped her arms and looked up at him. 'Thanks but it wasn't. I danced like a sack of potatoes. Sorry. Miles away.'

'We all have our off moments. Not that I go along with the sack of spuds. Shall we now face up to trifle or deep purple?'

Back at their table he beckoned their elderly waiter and having given the expected order laid a pound on the man's tray. 'I'd also like two shorts of anything you can find under the counter and no change.'

The note vanished. The waiter whispered, 'Do me best, sir. Can't promise. Much obliged, sir.' And he vanished.

'Fag in the interim, Caro?'

She looked at him for a couple of seconds. 'Thank you, doctor. I can use one.'

'You and me both, m'dear.' He used his blandest physician's voice. 'Yes, you're right. The doctor wants to talk to you. Time you snapped out of it.'

She raised her jaw. 'Of – what?'

He took it on the chin. 'How would I know? You haven't told me, Hoadley's no squealer and when did any grapevine get the facts right? All I know is misery when I see it and its a sight I don't enjoy.'

She was suddenly remorseful. 'Sam, I know you mean well and it's rude and unfair to slap you down after –'

'Stuff that!' The low voice was sharp as rifle fire. 'One of the many things I've enjoyed with you is the way you've ignored –'

'As my ex would say, knock it off, bud! All I meant was after all you took from me and did for Addie this afternoon.' She had spat back before she realized what she was saying. So bloody what? she thought. This is another first and last – he can have it. 'Yes. Would. Dick Dunlop's six foot deep version is off target, thank God, as he's a very good guy. Just back Stateside with the wife and kid. And no, he didn't lead me up the garden. I knew from square one, so yes, I had it coming! And I knew it from square one. That doesn't mean I have to like it, or that it stopped my loving him. Now, please, can I get off the couch?'

He acknowledged all she had just said with a slight gesture of one hand. He refused to use words; he knew there were none that would not give her what he considered justifiable offence. No matter how much she resented his silence, it would infuriate her less than the sympathy he longed to express but knew she would take, at best as pity, and worst, patronizing. He could see she deeply resented his having forced her confidence, and though the giving was probably providing some measure of relief, she would not forgive him on that score. He had been the recipient of too many confidences – the vast majority unforced – to have any illusions about the thankless role of the very often unwilling receiver.

A taut, hostile silence enveloped their table like a glass bowl; it was obvious she had no intention of helping to shatter the glass. He was searching his mind for a way through when their waiter's return and what followed almost immediately introduced the element of farce that in their present situation had only two outlets, tears or laughter, with the choice coming from characters.

'Best I could do, sir.' The waiter, with practised discretion, slid two napkin-covered, half-filled liqueur glasses from tray to table. 'Only Bourbon, I'm afraid, sir. Wouldn't know proper Scotch if we saw it, would we? But the guv'nor's got the drop of Bourbon left over from the Yanks and if you and your young lady's wanting coffee, best to order now. Milk's run out and coffee's getting on the low side. Two blacks after the sweet? Much obliged, sir!'

The man was turning away when the lights suddenly returned to a cacophony of jeers, boos and yells of 'Put out that light! Don't you know there's a peace on?'

For a second or two they blinked at each other across the table and then, in unison, shouted with laughter.

7

'I'll say this for George. When he's in action this room's the one warm spot in the Hut.' Hoadley's tone was abstracted as his gaze anatomically quartered the autoclave so named by Repairs and Works when they put it up in 1941. (An autoclave was a machine that sterilized with steam at high temperatures.) The one he was watching was long pre-war and looked rather like an outsize silver torpedo-tube on long, thin, steel rubber-footed legs. He straddled the room's only high wooden stool and mopped his face with the white cotton mask he had forgotten was round his throat when ending his morning ward rounds ten minutes ago.

'First day of spring due before this week ends, another three inches last night and more snow forecast. Someone's got their lines crossed. When are you going to shout "torpedoes away!", Nurse Carr?'

'Any second, Mr East.' Caroline's flushed, masked face did not turn from the gauges; it was one of that machine's several idiosyncrasies to overheat suddenly for no discoverable mechanical reason and the tins of rubber gloves it was presently sterilizing were needed for this afternoon's theatre-list. Rubber was still so short that every intact pair of gloves was treated like gold-dust, as only those could be used in the theatre proper. Mended gloves were used in the plaster-theatre, and by the nurses when doing the daily cleaning that involved using strong carbolic solution by the gallon.

Hoadley grunted and directed his abstracted gaze at the green-rubbered floor. Dick Dunlop, licking another label, glanced from Caroline's back to Hoadley, then shot another covertly anxious glance at Lindsay Kilbride and chancing to catch her eye, winked cheerfully. He was sticking upon the newly sterilized drums of dressings, gowns and towels the labels Lindsay was dating, timing and identifying. The hot drums were lined on a bare metal stretcher-trolley and had just been removed from the autoclave when the men came in to await Sister Theatre's return after hearing from the senior of the two student nurses making stock (dressings) in the open-doored stock-room off the main corridor, that a few minutes earlier Sister Theatre had been unexpectedly summoned to the Deputy Matron's office and that Nurse Carr was autoclaving. The men had come for the customary pre-list discussion with Sister Theatre of the list starting at 2 p.m. Hoadley had received the message with, 'Thanks, nurse.' Dick, standing a little behind, had winked at the girl, and knowing the department's accoustics trailed after the SSO in silence and once in the autoclave room started licking labels. His habit of helping the nurses with their routine jobs whenever he could was so well established that even Sister Theatre, an ardent upholder of etiquette, had come to regard as unexceptional the sight of the boyish, curly-haired RA cutting gauze rolls into dressing squares, rolling cotton wool balls into 'sponges', testing and mending gloves, or wearing oven-type gloves to heave around hot tins and drums. Being an autonomous department, once the rigorous daily cleaning was over, when the theatre proper was empty, stock-making, glove-testing and mending, packing tins and drums and autoclaving were the theatre nurses predominant non-stop occupations.

Being gregarious Dick enjoyed lending a hand, and recently, particularly when Lindsay was involved. Up to just over an hour ago he had thought all he had taken was a mild shine to her that would fade a couple of days after he left for National Service next month. And then he had chanced to be alone with the SSO when the SMO stopped them on the main ramp with an item of professional news that had not later needed the SSO's 'Covers down till this breaks, Dick'. Dick, muttering, 'Yes sir,' had been shaken by the depths of his immediate anxiety for Lindsay. For these last few minutes he had had consciously to assume his normal cheerful air, and when casting glances at Lindsay's curvacious figure especially suited by the ordinary uniform she, as all the theatre nurses, had on this morning, he had kept reminding himself of his private maxim that the physician who was not a born Jeremiah had yet to be born.

Lindsay was aware and mildly pleased by his interest, mainly as it seemed to her to illustrate that she had been Theatre 1 long enough to have crossed the greatest of all invisible barriers, that between the trained and untrained. She had been Theatre 1 from her return from quarantine nearly four weeks ago, and being now over her three months theatre-time, secretly hoped she was being kept on to assess her possibilities as a future theatre staff nurse. She was right about this. Formerly, Sister Theatre had had Nurse Jones in mind as Caroline's successor, chiefly, as Pat Jones had the more extrovert temperament, a small bosom and narrow hips. Sister Theatre liked 'a jolly gel' and distrusted, until proved mistaken, all those nurses she mentally termed 'the pouter pigeons' on the grounds that nothing must be allowed to disturb her surgeons' concentration; surgeons were men and men were men. But she was a fair-minded woman, and after Lindsay's first week as Theatre 1, had confided to Caroline without humour – Sister Theatre lacked that sense – that Kilbride was shaping very nicely and it just proved once more what a good training and responsibility could do for a gel. Caroline had agreed, then added unusually, 'Actually Sister, I've thought Kilbride a born theatre nurse since she joined us.' The rider was unusual, as previously Caroline had agreed without qualification with Sister Theatre – the surest way for a quiet working life for all theatre nurses and surgeons.

It had been Caroline's desperate need for a quiet life that had made her accept her present post despite the demotion and drop in pay to £8 a month (all found). One letter of application could have got her a ward sister's job elsewhere in this country or overseas. She had not wanted to go elsewhere or pack another kitbag. She had wanted to crawl back to the known security of her parent hospital and to the stringently ordered routine of theatre work with its constant demand for emotional detachment and its long, often irregular hours that would leave little time for a private life or insomnia. The TD had provided all and more than she had sought; action was the enemy of thought and her always active working life had given her the unconscious comfort of doing an highly skilled, essential job. She had made a mess of her private life, but she was not wasting her life and not even her sense of personal inferiority could dint her professional certainty that her existence was necessary to others. The patients' needs were non-stop, whether in the aseptic conditions of the theatre proper, or the hard work in the background that was vital to maintain those conditions. Though penicillin was now in general use and its anti-sepsis properties were revolutionizing medicine and surgery, the danger of theatre-induced sepsis remained the fear the TD dreaded second only to a death on the operating table. It was Sister Theatre's pride that not once since she opened her department in the Hut, had it had to be closed for fumigation consequent on theatre-induced sepsis. Some of that pride had rubbed off on Caroline and as the months in her new job raced by she had achieved a content that she had only properly appreciated in retrospect during her long weekend in London last month. It had been after that insight that she had discovered how much the dip outbreak had disturbed that content, and how still more disturbing had been that Saturday afternoon and evening with Sam.

When their dinner-date ended he had taken her back to the principal's house, collected his overnight bag, said no more than good manners demanded – which didn't include the pretence of 'We must do this again some other time' – and removed himself to the one of his clubs that he said had a night porter. She had still been too angry for anything but relief. Hindsight had since turned that anger upon herself for wrecking his evening and her remorse had been deepened by Addie's telling her on their drive to lunch the next day, that Sam's brother had gone down with his ship in the Atlantic in 1943. She was sure – rightly – this had been an additional reason for Sam's silent disapproval of her behaviour to MacNab. When it comes to putting up blacks, she had thought, sure as hell do I take the cookie. And that thought had provoked a prolonged mental stock-taking that was beginning to show on and off-duty. She had seen nothing of Sam in the first and little in the second, from that Saturday night. When they met in queues at the serving-hatches in the dining-room they exchanged polite smiles, and in the grounds, exaggerated shivers. The lingering bitter weather gave him more than one excuse for hurrying on his way; it was causing such widespread local bronchitis and pneumonia, that Arumchester General's medical wards had up extra beds and a good proportion of the Hut's medical beds were now filled with local patients.

Sister Theatre was affronted by her rider on Kilbride. 'Why have you not told me this previously, nurse? Training and assessing our student nurses and reporting your findings to me is part of your job.'

'I'm sorry, Sister. I – I expect I needed to think about it.'

'Oh. Possibly. Well, then, let's deal with tomorrow's list. We start at 9 a.m. with three 'clean' orthopods – that will please Mr East! He really relishes bone-surgery, but this is a general theatre and he is appointed as a general surgeon, as he has to turn his hand to whatever is presented – yes, three orthopods, two VVs (Varicose veins), then the RIH (Right Inguinal Hernia), and the two "cold" appendices. I shall take the first five, you'll take the hernia and first appendix, and then I'll let Kilbride take the second. I shall be at her side and will pre-inform Mr East that she will be presiding over her first instruments' trolley.'

Lindsay had taken that appendicectomy with the efficiency of an experienced instruments' nurse and evoked a 'Thank you very much, Nurse Kilbride. First-rate,' from the SSO that had endeared him to her for life. Other results had been a gracious nod from Sister Theatre and the onset of the most halcyon period in Lindsay's training. She had always loved and sensed her natural aptitude for theatre work, but being both shy of her seniors and a loyal friend, and having discerned – as nurses always do – that Pat was Sister's pet, she had intentionally kept in the professional background. Then the combination of the removal of her dread of Pat's spreading dip through her clandestine love-life, her own secret fear of getting it and her relief that the medical bulletins on all four in Badgers Heath were continuously satisfactory that had accompanied her return to duty, had made her rise to her promotion with the instinctive assurance of someone doing the right job in the right place. And on her first day back Caroline had used their first opportunity for a private conversation to say, 'You were right to tell me what you did, Kilbride, but no more sweat there. Flap over, QED. I've kept what you said to myself.'

'Thanks awfully, nurse. Did you – er do you,' their eyes met, 'or shouldn't I ask?'

'Old history. Let it go.'

'Och, yes. Thanks again,' said Lindsay, thankfully dismissing from her mind the unknown boyfriend that her strong sense of nationalism now refused to identify as 'Jock', in the reasonable certainty that by now Pat had replaced him with Badgers Heath's one resident houseman, an ex-Free Polish Army MO whom the Hut grapevine insisted (no one enquired how) looked like a haunted Clark Gable, and who had not gone back to his wife and home in Poland as neither had survived for him to return to. The poor bod but needs a streak of the wolf to be Pat's type, decided Lindsay, until she's discharged home for a long sick leave and falls hard for the next.

She now replaced her fountain pen in her dress bib pocket and pulled down the mask she was only wearing as an anti-steam protection. 'These drums are cool enough to put away, Nurse Carr.'

'Good.' Caroline kept one eye on the gauges whilst pulling off one oven glove to flick out her watch. It was five to eleven and they had both had their free ten-to-ones altered to eleven-to-twos to finish the autoclaving. 'Get them into the drum-room, bring back that trolley, then go off, nurse. If Sister's not back by eleven I'll tell her I sent you.'

Hoadley looked up. 'Dunlop'll bring back the trolley, nurse. Shut that door after you, lad. I'm warm for the first time since God knows when.'

'Yessir.'

In the aftermath of the rumbling, jangling trolley the whirrs of the extractor fans in the ceiling were much louder. 'Any idea why the Dep. Mat.'s scrounged Sister, Caro?'

She shook her head at the quivering needles. 'Probably just flapping about Ferdie and Prof. Surgery coming down for this afternoon's list. She – hold everything! Stop that, George!' She thumped the machine with a gloved hand. 'Spit it out!' Another thump and the safety-valve on the rounded topside simultaneously emitted a piercing whistle and jet of boiling steam. 'That's the form. Temp. dropping nicely.'

Hoadley, momentarily diverted, growled, 'Give him a tepid sponge-down.'

'Repairs and Works wouldn't approve.' She gestured to-wards the thickly rubbered flex trailing to a special plug in the skirting board. '"Blow George and you blow the Hut, nurse. Just give him a good bash and he'll work a treat." He does too, unless cooking gloves. Must be the smell that puts him off. The tins are identical with the ones we use for emergency blood and drip settings. Pack him with gloves and turn your back and he shoots a temp that reduces the lot to smelly brown jelly and sends Sister through the roof. I wish rubber would start coming back. Having to cosset every pair is getting me down. Bad as Normandy.'

'Cut the natter. Gen coming off the record whilst we're alone.'

'Hold on. Got to turn off.' She dealt with the controls and as the temperature had to fall before the machine could be opened, she turned curiously. He was sitting with his great shoulders hunched and strong squarish hands resting on his thick thighs as she had seen him sitting around in this and other theatres upon innumerable occasions, and she knew at once from the lack of expression in his heavy face that the gen was bad. 'Spit it out, Hoadley.'

He looked at her. 'Odds on what the Dep. Mat.'s telling Sister. Nurse Jones.'

She stared. 'Jones? Complications?' He nodded. 'Cardiac? Any paralysis?'

'Yep. Evan Evans had a call from Badgers' on the pundits' "outside" just after nine-thirty. Their Med. Super had already rung London to call in Ferdie. Wires red hot and the latest gen I've had is that a taxi'll be waiting for Ferdie at Arumchester at ten to twelve and take him straight to her. He'll then come on here and, if he's not in time for Miss Granton, Evan'll give her anaesthetic.'

She nodded briefly at that last item that was established procedure in these particular circumstances. Miss Granton, the first patient on this afternoon's list, had an abdominal cancer and was a long-retired, former Sister Stanley Parker. It was a Martha's tradition that present and retired members of the staff having major operations were operated upon and anaesthetized by senior members of the teaching Staff, or their most senior deputies.

She said slowly. 'God, I'm sorry. I thought the poor kid was doing nicely.'

'She was until early this morning. Heart suddenly started playing up. Tough break.'

'Hideously tough.' She had to turn back to the machine. 'I've got to open. Turn your back and get your hands under cover.' She glanced back to ensure he had, then carefully turned the large steel wheel controlling the three inch thick circular steel door. Immediately the latch released purchase the safety-valve, whistled the warning that the door was loose, and before easing it open she ducked to the side of its protection and turned her head away. A second later the belching clouds of steam misted the whole room before being sucked upwards by the fans. 'He must cool more before I can disembowel.' She turned back to Hoadley as he swung round on the stool. 'The heart-block can be transient. Or is there myocardial damage?'

'Evan didn't specify. Ferdie'll tell us.'

'Thank God he was coming down. Save some time. But –' she broke off. 'Here's the trolley.'

He got up to open the door for the trolley that was pushed in alone by Sister Theatre.

Sister Theatre was a slight, neat-featured woman in the early forties but looked older as she had never used anything but soap and water on her face and wore her fading brown hair in the fashion insisted upon for all Martha's nurses up to the outbreak of the Second World War. This was dragged back from a centre-parting into a tight bun or roll high on the back of the head. She apologized with abnormal severity for keeping Mr East waiting and asking Mr Dunlop to remain outside until summoned. Normally her attitude to surgeons was that of an indulgent mother to her sometimes tiresome, often foolish, but always lovable little children. And then her severe glance fell upon the empty stool as if to her it was no inanimate object but represented an emotional necessity. Hoadley, exchanging a quick, guarded glance with Caroline, pushed it forward. 'Won't you sit down, Sister?'

'Thank you, Mr East.' She sat straight-backed, folded her hands in her lap, looked from one to the other and said in her brisk and most professionally impersonal voice, 'I am extremely sorry to have to tell you both that our Nurse P. M. Jones died in Badgers Heath at ten-thirty-five this morning. Cardiac failure. Nothing could be done. A message to this effect is now awaiting Dr Fenton at Arumchester. Presumably, he will come on with Professor Surgery as previously anticipated.'

Hoadley muttered incoherently and Caroline, audibly, 'Sister, I am so sorry.'

'We are all most distressed. The Deputy Matron will tell the day nursing staff at lunchtime. Dr Evans is with her now, Mr

East, and knowing you to be awaiting my return the Deputy Matron trusts you will forgive her delegating this to me.' He inclined his head. 'Very sad. Very distressing. We all know only too well these tragic events occur, but –' suddenly her voice shed the professional impersonality, 'when it occurs to someone so young, of so much promise and in previous good health – such a jolly gel –' and she could say no more.

They looked at each other over her lowered, befrilled head and in their momentarily unguarded faces was the same despair at their familiarity with this moment. Neither could possibly have numbered the times they had had to receive this kind of news and accept that too often neither youth nor health were an armour against bullets, shrapnel, falling masonry, flames, starvation or the diseases that could kill.

Caroline, looking away first and down at the floor, thought numbly, we're tougher than Sister. We've had to be. Not Sister. She's spent the last twenty years in theatres without her own patients, so she has not had to watch some of them die. She had no male relatives on active service; her only brother was 'reserved', her father too old; and she's never had the time to take in much of what was going on outside her department. Hoadley and I were pitched into it and had to take it or crack and somehow we didn't, at least, not outwardly. Probably that was as another thing the war forced was an outward show of the courage that's vital for survival and that show became a conditional reflex. On the outside. On the inside, every time, first something turned numb then later sloughed off like dead skin from an old wound, leaving another scar. Too much has had to slough off in both of us. I could weep for that poor kid – only I can't. No tears left. Nor has he. So we're both dry-eyed as hell. Not Sister, though any second training'll dry her eyes and she'll start talking about the list.

'Do forgive me, Mr East.' Sister blew her nose, Hoadley groaned compassionately and she stepped from the stool and stood straight-backed. 'We must attend to the list, but I must first send off Nurse Carr. I'll finish the gloves, nurse, but before you go just ring Repairs and Works about the third sterilizer. I was about to do so when the Office rang and most reprehensibly, it slipped my mind.'

'Yes, Sister.' (And that's not all you've forgotten, honey.) 'Sister, I've sent off Nurse Kilbride, but as Nurse Jones was in her set, shouldn't I tell her before she hears the official announcement at lunch?'

'Oh. Yes, yes would you? I dislike asking this – yes, naturally you understand. Thank you, nurse. I'll have a little talk with the nurses in the stock-room very shortly. Shall we remain in this warmth, Mr East?'

'Infinitely preferable, Sister. Send in Dunlop, please Nurse Carr.' He opened the door for her and neither looked at the other as she went by and before the door closed heard his, 'Snow still seems to be holding off, Sister.'

The autoclave-room lay beyond the small plaster-theatre that was off the far end of the anaesthetic room. The far end and corridor doors of the last were hooked open and the murmurs of Dick's conversation with the stock-making Theatres 3 and 5 filtered from the stock-room that was two down from the duty-room. Having dispatched Dick without noticing that he too had avoided looking at her, Caroline asked Nurse Stevens, Theatre 3, to make tea with the kettle she was about to put on. 'I've got to make a phone call before I go off, Stevens. Use the big pot, five teaspoons, take it into Sister and say I said so.'

The nurses were delighted. They sat on either side of a narrow trestle table with cloaks pushed back from their shoulders and scarlet theatre blankets wrapped round from the waist down, respectively cutting a roll of gauze into twelve-inch lengths and folding the lengths into quadrupled squares with all outer edges on the insides. Mid-morning tea, when there was no list, was an undreamed-of luxury. The department's special tea ration was four ounces a week and the standard routine two teaspoons in a small pot. Obviously Carr intended them to be in on this party and when she vanished to the duty-room but not out of earshot, they mouthed their joy at the prospective buckshee cuppas.

'Repair and Works. Foreman, here.'

'I'm glad it's you, Mr Henty. Nurse Carr. Theatre.'

Mr Henty sighed. 'I might've known. What is it now, nurse?'

'Our third instruments' sterilizer has suddenly gone U/S. We don't know why. Please could someone look at it this morning? We've a major list starting at two and the theatre proper'll be closed for setting from one.'

'I dunno, Nurse Carr. I do not know when I've known the theatre not wanting the job done yesterday. You theatre young ladies seem to think we got nothing but the theatre on our books. Ah, well, have to sort it. I tell you what, Nurse Carr, if I can't step up myself a little after half-eleven I'll fetch young Bert up by twelve and he'll have to take his dinner-break late. We'll sort it.'

Caroline said mechanically, 'Mr Henty, you're an angel.'

'That's not what my lads call me, nurse,' he retorted smiling to himself as he put down.

Caroline sat back in the chair and closing her eyes, began untying her mask. She could always see reality more clearly with her eyes shut and she saw with dreadful clarity the chain of isolated, pointless events that had ended in the tragic waste of a girl's life. It was long as established as it could ever be that she had caught dip upon that Thursday in London and in some unknown manner given it to Simon Phillips. In Badgers Heath and the Hut, the physicians had been united in their opinion that upon his admission to the fevers' hospital Phillips had been at a more advanced stage than Miss Yelton and Mr Mathers. There had been no other medical explanation for this; events had apparently proved it, even though, (according to the Hut grapevine) Phillips continued to insist he had had no contact with Pat Jones. Just something else to be accepted, thought Caroline numbly, grimacing in self-disgust. I can see the tragedy – I just can't feel it. I'm not just toughened, I'm cauterized – all feelings gone. I'll have to do something about this, or this is how I'll stay and I'll turn into one of those bitchy sisters that tell juniors to stop dramatizing and making spectacles of themselves when the poor kids weep in linen-rooms after a patient dies. I'll have to do something – I've got to snap out of it – only I can't think how – not now – no time – that kettle – and Kilbride – oh God – what can I say to the poor kid?

'What?' Her mind whiplashed the question and answer. You know damn well what! You've got the hideous form taped. Rep. Mist., woman. Rep. Mist.! (*Repitita Mistura* – the mixture as before.)

She jerked open her eyes and saw Sam watching her from the open doorway. He had just come in and left his tea-cosy and boots by the ramp doors and his two pairs of socks had muffled his footsteps. He had heard the duty-room telephone being put down as he came in, and on exchanging smiles with the nurses in the stock-room seen they had not yet heard the news that would cast a deep shadow over the entire day staff before first lunch was over. He had just had it from the SMO on the ramp, who had then sent him here with a message for Hoadley. He had expected Caroline to be off-duty as it was Friday morning before Sister Theatre's alternate free weekend when her staff nurses invariably had a ten-to-one. He had hoped for both their sakes that she was off; for Caroline's, as it would give her a little private time between the announcement and returning to a TD plunged into communal grief; for himself, as where she was concerned abstinence had become his only solution and he was deeply saddened by Pat Jones's death. He had taken this news with his customary quietude and the same sense of that terrible despair that had been momentarily in Caroline and Hoadley's unguarded faces in the autoclave-room, and that had returned to linger in her closed-eyed face when he saw her sitting at the duty-room desk.

The telephone rang before he had time to explain or she to ask, why he was there. 'I can wait, nurse.'

'Thanks . . . Theatre. Nurse Carr.'

'I hoped you'd not gone seeing I just heard you with Mr Henty, Nurse Carr.' June, one of the local girl operatives on the Hut's day switchboard, sounded perturbed. 'I know I'm not meant to put through outside calls to nurses on-duty, but shouldn't you be off, nurse?'

'Yes. Just leaving. Outside call for me? London?'

'No, nurse. Bread Street and –'

'Bread Street?' Caroline cut in. This was a village eleven miles from Ash where she knew no one.

'Yes, nurse. Mr Weaver's number and Mr Martin calling from there and wanting the word with you special. Mr Martin MacNab, I should say, nurse, and he says to say he'll be ever so grateful if you can spare the moment. What'll I do, nurse?'

She shot Sam the first helpless glance he had seen from her and her lips framed 'MacNab! He's heard!' Then her face went blank. 'Put him through, please, June.'

'Ta, nurse.' She heard the clicks on the line and Sam, watching her keenly, the click in his mind that released a stored and unanswered question based solely on clinical intuition. 'Through to Nurse Carr in theatre now, Mr Martin.'

'Bless you, Junie! Martin MacNab here, Staff Nurse Carr and a very good morning to you!' His pleasant voice had the patently artificial note of someone speaking in the presence or hearing of others at his end. 'Old Tom Ford's boss – and I know you'll be glad to hear old Tom's living the life of Reilly resting up down Widdington way. Do forgive my barging in like this, but my wife and I were so grateful for your good advice over getting our boys jabbed I hope you won't mind my trying to scrounge a spot more. Can't get hold of old Doc Yardley – he's out of signal range delivering a sprog miles off – and I know your chaps can't hand out advice on other chaps' unseen patients – so yours was the name that sprang most charmingly to mind. Do hope you don't object?'

Her intelligence had taken over. She knew the difference in the sounds of a man shooting a line and a man pretending to do so. And you're too smooth not to know it too, she thought rapidly, and too bright to ask what I was dreading with an audience that almost certainly includes June. She said evenly, 'Mr NacNab, I'm a nurse not a doctor, so not qualified to give medical advice. But why do you need it?'

'Knew you'd rally, Staff Nurse!' He laughed artifically. 'This is the set-up – I've just run over to Bread Street to drop off some milk churns and stopped in to leave a message about our next shoot with the glamorous wife of one of my old oppos, Henry Weaver, and found poor old Henry too under the weather to go into his office in Arumchester today. Poor chap's luck's been out lately –' he rattled on 'couple of weeks or so back he bunged a pickaxe through his foot shifting snow. Not much of a stab – boot took most – but damned sore only old Henry's the stoic type so it took Peggy – Mrs Henry – a couple of days to persuade him to let old Yardley look at it. Too late to bung in the odd stitch, but the old boy doused it with penicillin powder and gave him the odd shots and said to let him know if it gave any more trouble and old Henry vows it hasn't. Only this morning he's feeling rather ropey and – bit of a laugh this – having quite a dodgy time getting down his elevenses' cuppa. I've just suggested driving him up for your chaps to look at, but he's ag'in it and says if he doesn't feel better he'll give Yardley a buzz tomorrow. Like I said – stoic type. But as yours truly is the type that never hesitates to slip in the unwanted oar – scars to prove it! – I've twisted his arm to let me use his blower and ask what you think?'

She had listened intently and Sam had seen a reminiscent warning light flare in her lovely, intelligent eyes. She said, 'Am I right in thinking he can hear you?'

'Bullseye.'

'Has he ever had mumps?'

'Yes.'

'This difficulty in swallowing – has he got a stiff neck and is he having trouble opening his mouth properly and getting his chin down?'

'Bang on!'

Sam was much closer and stooping to listen to both sides of the conversation.

'Those odd shots – penicillin and Anti-Tetanus Serum?'

'Yes. That's what's foxing –'

'Can be confusing.' She cut him short, gently. And in the same tone said, 'What I think, Mr MacNab, is that you should drive him up to our Casualty with the utmost dispatch.'

From his quick intake of breath he understood her use of the Navy's most urgent message, but it didn't show in his voice. 'Good show! May give me the chance to see you. Oh – knowing how all establishments cherish the old bumf – Henry Weaver's my solicitor – for his sins – my age, 36, and back in the dark ages we were at school together. Thanks a bundle, Staff Nurse! Good to talk to you again. Cheers!' He rang off.

She did the same, looking up at Sam. 'How much did you get?'

He was frowning in thought. 'Most.'

She got up, filled the kettle at the hand-basin and plugged it in. 'And –?'

'Wondering why you aren't in medicine.'

'You don't have to be once you've nursed tetanus.'

He looked at her sharply. 'To recovery?' She nodded. 'How often?'

'Just twice. Our own troops. Different times, same posting. I'd night-specialled the first, so got the second.'

He was very impressed. He had never seen a surviving case of tetanus. 'Use curare?'

'No. The physicians said it was too much of an additional risk to the respiratory muscles.'

'What did you use?'

She told him briefly, succinctly.

'How did you get in enough calories?'

'First and last by mouth. Nasal tube in between. Try and set up a drip, either you spark off a spasm or the next snaps the needle. My pair had bad spasms but luckily, marvellously strong hearts. They did all right, eventually.'

That wasn't their only luck, he thought, but this was not the moment to say so. He had now recalled the whole present and so, he saw, had she. He glanced into the corridor, saw the hovering nurse, and said only, 'I'm looking for the SSO, Nurse Carr. *In situ?*'

'The autoclave-room, Dr Lincoln Browne. Sorry you had to wait.'

'That's all right.' He stepped aside to let her go out first. She disappeared into the nurses' changing-room, he into the an-aesthetic-room, and Nurse Stevens, after checking the kettle's warmth, ducked back to the stock-room to compare notes on what they had severally just overheard and bewail the fact that she had not been born sooner.

'I wish I'd had Carr's luck and been old enough to be in the war! I've never heard of anyone but aged types like Home Sister and Sister Flo actually nursing tetanus. They had oodles in the Great War – hardly any last show. All the same it must have been terrific fun nursing in all the blood and muck! Trust me to miss out on the war and end up in this icy, manless wilderness, goose-pimples all over.' She massaged her bare fore-arms. 'I promise you this, when I finish training nothing, but NOTHING, is keeping my lamp burning in England! I'm toting it to foreign parts and the sun – oh, kettle's not boiling yet, Nurse Carr.'

'My fault for putting it on late.' In the doorway, Caroline slung her coat over her greatcoat. 'When you take in the tray, Stevens, will you tell Sister Repairs and Works'll be up by noon? Thanks.'

She walked on quickly and out into the bitter cold that still iced the ramps, fringed roofs with icicles, and hardened to grey chunks the swept back snow on Casualty Yard and up the drive. She did not notice the external temperature nor stop until passing her own Home. She went swiftly into her cubicle and, though nurses were forbidden to smoke in uniform, she took from a drawer an opened blue-paper-wrapped packet of ten Players, a box of matches and the two bread rolls she had saved from yesterday's bread ration to give the birds when she was off this morning.

She had seen no birds when she went indoors, but within seconds of her continuing path to the Third-Year Home, she was surrounded by a flapping brown and black cloud, swoop-ing, jostling and fighting for every crumb. Tamed by hunger, falsely fattened by cold, they brushed against her body, got between her feet and with that peculiarly acute observation that so often accompanies acute anxiety, she identified, jays, chaffinches, rooks, blackbirds, robins, magpies and a solitary heron before she went in and called from the outer bathrooms' corridor. 'Nurse Kilbride? Nurse Carr. May I come in please?'

It was nearly one o'clock when she came out again and from the crest of the snowbank hiding the bare hedge that backed the wooden line of dormitory huts, the birds huddled in puffed-out, bedraggled groups, watched her with beady hungry eyes and stayed motionless. She did not see them. On her own doorstep she stamped off snow, then walked slowly as an old woman to her own cubicle and still in her outdoor things sat on the side of her bed and with shaking hands took out and lit the last cigarette in the crumpled packet. And then the sudden klaxon of the ringing telephone in the outer corridor jarred every nerve she possessed. She raced to silence the noise, and felt so deathly tired she needed a conscious effort to speak, 'Staff Nurses. Nurse Carr.'

'Lincoln Browne, nurse.' His voice was curt. 'Sorry to bother you, but did you inadvertently pick up one of those notes I put on your duty-room desk when I came in for the SSO? A page is missing that I need, and I've just remembered seeing you putting a memo in your apron bib. Is my lost page stuck to it?'

The speed of her response surprised neither as both had spent years in hospitals. 'I'll check, doctor – yes – I did – I'm sorry. You want it now? Where'll you be?'

'Just leaving Flo for the Path Lab. Thanks.' The line went dead.

She had suspended thought and curiosity. She stubbed out her cigarette in the nearest sand bucket and went straight out. He was waiting by the coke stack behind Casualty when she reached the Yard. He was not wearing the tea-cosy, and had a file of notes under one arm and both hands in his greatcoat pockets. The sun had just broken through the parchment overcast and though the sunlight had no warmth it had the brightness of early spring that with the snowlight gave a brilliant clarity. Walking up to him she noticed with the same acuteness as with the birds, that he was now looking as he had by candlelight last month.

'Why the cloak-and-dagger, Sam?'

'To get in my apology before –'

'You don't owe –'

'I do. Please shut up,' he said, 'please, and listen. You're going back on nights tonight to special Weaver in Flo SW3 – just fixed. You'll hear soon enough.' She was looking up at him blankly. 'You did more than a very snappy spot of diagnosing on him. I had to tell Evan the lot, he had to tell Ferdie, and Ferdie went straight to the Dep. Mat. to ask for you.' She still said nothing. 'We'd had to put Weaver in Flo as it's the only place in the Hut where he can get the essential quiet. Sister Theatre and Sister Flo have both been up in arms, but Sister Flo's coming round having nursed tetanus *ad nauseam* last time round.' He hesitated. 'Sorry I had to turn squealer, Caro.'

'You had to.' She too hesitated. 'The Office probably tried to contact me whilst I was with Kilbride.'

'Probably. How is she?'

'As you'd expect.'

'And you?'

'Ditto.' She looked at his right shoulder. 'How about you?'

'Snap.'

She nodded at his shoulder. 'Thanks for this alert and the apology.'

'Thanks for taking both, stat.,' he said to the top of her shawled head. Throughout this meeting there had been others passing but the shadow had fallen and none had bothered to look up from the ground. He glanced back at her pale, drawn, tired, lovely face.

'I hope you get some sleep this afternoon.' He turned away and went on to the Path Lab.

She was crossing the Yard to the drive when one of the Office Sisters called to her from the entrance to Admin. 'There you are, Nurse Carr! I've just been ringing your Home for you.

The Deputy Matron would like to see you in her Office now, please – just as you are, nurse. The Deputy Matron will understand.'

8

If Caroline had not just heard from Sam that Henry Weaver
was worse, she would have known it directly she opened the
duty-room door. Mrs Weaver was slumped in the armchair
that for the last fifty-odd hours had been moved into Small
Ward 3 and, when she saw who had come in, an expression of
reluctant relief momentarily overcame the immediate hostility
in her ravaged face.

Sam, the acting-SMO from lunchtime yesterday, had been
in and out of Florence by day and night from Friday afternoon. He came out of the ramp door as Caroline walked up
the side ramp to report on-duty for her third night and in the
rays of the overhead light now left on all night, she saw at once
what had happened. There was no one else around, so she
said, 'Spasms started.'

'First, an hour ago.' He went on to explain quickly as he
was needed in Charity. Finally, he said, 'For God's sake, Caro,
pack in the glucose . . . if you can,' and walked on quickly.
She stopped only to change her boots for her uniform shoes,
then went in, quickly, silently. Neither of them had noticed
Sam was capless and wore his greatcoat over his shoulders,
that Caroline's shawl was draped round her neck and not
face, not that the icicle fringes were pockmarking the snow
with slow, heavy drops.

She came silently into the duty-room, boots under one arm,

empty shoebag and two spare clean aprons under the other and closed the door before saying 'Good evening, Mrs Weaver,' and, as she expected, getting back a curt 'Evening, nurse.' Previously, she had always got on well with the next-of-kin of DILs, all of whom had recognized nearly as swiftly as her patients that she was fighting on their side. Mrs Weaver had not left Florence since Friday afternoon and had come to treat the rest of the nursing staff and the itinerant pundits and residents as old friends – and to be so treated by them – but though she had not now seen Caroline since the first few hours of Friday night her attitude to her husband's night-special remained as then. And then, it had gone from frigid civility to open rudeness.

Caroline's initial reaction to Mrs Weaver's icy reception had been as wholly sympathetic as the one she had had for her very similar reception from the night staff when she arrived in the dining-room for 8.15 p.m. 'breakfast'. There had been a change-over on nights since she was last on; most of the night nurses and all three of the then suddenly enlarged Florence night staff were strangers to her. And that night the entire staff had been stunned by waking to the news of Pat Jones's death. Even the normally serene Mrs Ames had looked grave, older, and merely nodded when Caroline, sitting with the Night Sisters at the high table, passed on the news of Miss Granton she had just had from Home Sister. 'Op couldn't have gone better, all out, she's round and asking Sister Vic for a nice cup of tea.' The new Night Ass. muttered something about Miss Granton being one of the old school and proving it by de-manding a general bed in Vic and refusing a Flo small ward as Vic was nearer the theatre, and there all conversation ended.

And in SW3, Mrs Weaver, whom Caroline judged about Mrs Ames's age, had looked a large, untidy, stunned and fright-ened schoolgirl. Caroline had been very sorry for her, and guessed – rightly – that Mrs Weaver had never before seen dangerous illness nor been in a great voluntary hospital. Terrifying for her, thought Caroline. This morning her husband woke with what she thought was just a stiff neck;

tonight he's on the DIL in a curtained-off small ward in a women's ward, with a staff nurse permanently at his bedside, Sister Flo, senior student nurses, men in black jackets and long and short white coats coming and going non-stop, the Dep. Mat. in twice oozing authority and soothing smiles, and all of us moving in slow-motion, never talking unless essential or above a murmur. On top of all this she's bound to be worried sick about the two little daughters she's had to leave with the MacNabs at their farm until her mother arrives from Leicester tomorrow and takes her grandchildren back to their home in Bread Street.

Caroline had known all this from Sister Flo's day report and when, around midnight, leaving Nurse Shaw, the night senior, in temporary charge of her sleeping patient, and using sign-language coaxed Mrs Weaver from her armchair and across the corridor into the duty-room, she said kindly, 'You should try and get some sleep now, Mrs Weaver. The bed in SW1 is ready for you, hottie (hot water bottle) *in situ*, though I'm afraid a stone as we're out of rubber. How about a hot cuppa, first? Cocoa, malted milk, or would you prefer tea? If so, we've plenty tonight.'

Mrs Weaver flicked back her untidy, shoulder-length brown hair. 'You don't have to smarm, nurse. I'm not your patient and I'm not thirsty.'

Caroline was only momentarily taken aback. Twelve hours in hell was one hell of a long time. 'You'd like to go straight to bed.'

'Yes.' But she made no move and looked hard at Caroline's face. 'Aren't you the Staff Nurse Carr Martin MacNab rang from our house this morning?' Caroline nodded sensing what was coming was not gratitude. 'I thought you must be. He described you. You'd better know he happens to be my husband's greatest chum and Marigold MacNab is mine. We were at school together.'

Caroline smiled professionally. 'I'm glad. You'll feel much happier about leaving your daughters with such great friends. I'll just take you over –'

'I know my way and how to find the bathrooms. I don't

forget things. I won't make any noise. You'll call me at once if –'

'Of course, but I sincerely hope that won't be necessary and I'm fairly sure it won't.'

Mrs Weaver was a rather pretty young woman. She did not look pretty then. 'How can you be sure? You're only a nurse not a doctor so don't try and patronize me, my girl! I won't –' She was interrupted by Sam's opening the door for Dr Evans and her aggression dropped off like an old coat. 'Wanting me, doctors?' she breathed.

The men smiled reassuringly and when Sam closed the door, the SMO said, 'Just taking another look at your good man, Mrs Weaver, then looking in to bid you the good-night that from Mr Weaver's appearance should be yours. A word when you're free, Nurse Carr. No hurry, Mrs Weaver.'

'I'm just going to bed, doctor. I don't want nurse. Thank you, doctors – thank you both very much for all you are doing for my husband. Goodnight and God bless you both.'

Sam, closing the door after her, glanced sideways at Caroline's face that in Dick Dunlop's vernacular wore her hearing-the-bell-for-vespers expression. Then he leant against the door, folded his arms, and as had become his custom when standing around attending the SMO, pretended he was a fly on the wall. An elegant, watchful, silent fly.

Dr Evans said drily, 'One fact of hospital life that never ceases to astonish me is how frequently we chaps collect the undeserved plaudits.' He was a tallish thin man with a sharp, clever face and steel-rimmed glasses that he wore as often on his high forehead as upon his nose. He pushed them up to look quizzically at Caroline. 'One must remember she is a very anxious woman, and presumably, one might add blessedly, ignorant of the fact that she may yet have you to thank for saving her husband's life. It remains an open question whether we got him in time, but in my opinion there is no question that even a delay of a few more hours would have left no alternative to a fatal prognosis.'

'She's far too shocked to think clearly, Dr Evans.'

'True, nurse. Very true.'

Sam's indignation on her behalf forced him to break his self-imposed rule and voice it indirectly. 'She's very grateful to MacNab.'

She looked at him in not wholly concealed gratitude. 'She should be. He raised the alert, got Weaver here, and he and his wife are looking after the Weaver kids tonight, ringing the Office every few hours and sending with every message "not to worry, sprogs fine".' She smiled faintly. 'I had to translate "sprogs" to Sister Flo.'

Sam nodded non-committally. Dr Evans murmured with unusual triteness that one needed good friends in trying times, as he was suddenly longing for his wife who he would see again tomorrow afternoon and was the one person to whom he could confide the ambivalence of his feelings at having temporarily to hand over Weaver to a deputy whose medical competence equalled his own. He collected his thoughts to ask, 'What do you think of our patient, nurse?'

As neither man had known her specialling a DIL before, her reply professionally surprised and relieved both. 'Not too good. Could be worse, but not too good. On the good side, he's a strong, obviously very intelligent man in his prime and, as obviously, he's a fighter with a lot to fight for. On the other side –' she shook her head a little, 'he does not yet look to me as if those massive shots of antitoxin he's had since admission are having much – if any – effect on neutralizing the toxin that's already reached his central nervous system.' They nodded, watching her keenly. 'Another thing that's obvious, is that the bacilli have had time to multiply plus at the site of innoculation. When Mr East came in on his round tonight he told me the Path Lab have already found a particle of boot amongst the gubbins he excised when cleaning up that old stab wound in the left foot this afternoon. Pitchfork must have driven it in, he said, and if the spores were on it, they've had twenty-three days to cook, and a head-start of forty-eight hours before his first ATS (Anti-Tetanus Serum). Not too good.'

'Indeed. Having just come from the Path Lab we've heard

much the same from Dr Sumner. He's busy cooking cultures and convinced the particle of boot's the guilty party. He told us he doubts there's a pair of tetanus-free garden or farm boots in this county. Such good agricultural soil is heavy with the Clostridium tetani after centuries of farm animals and horses. Horses still in general use on farms – as indeed that chap MacNab was saying this afternoon. He told us his father had the first local tractor in the early '30s and that it was his recollection of an incident upon his father's farm at around that period that prompted him to ring you this morning.'

She was very curious. 'I've been wondering about that, Dr Evans.'

'Exercised our minds, nurse. MacNab gave no explanation till Mrs Weaver had left with her husband for this ward, to avoid alarming her further. It seems that in those times they were still harvesting by hand and during his school holidays it was his father's custom to send him down with a barrel of cider for the reapers at the end of each working day. One evening one unfortunate chap couldn't open his mouth to quaff his cider – much merriment all round – short-lived. Poor chap had gashed himself with his own scythe a week or so previously and done nothing much about it. Tetanus-infected. Died within the week. Hypostatic pneumonia from MacNab's description, wouldn't you say, Sam?'

'Yes, sir.' His eyes met Caroline's. 'MacNab said one look at Weaver this morning brought it all back. The rest you know, nurse.'

'Yes,' she said, unexpectedly reading in his dark eyes how much more he had guessed – or knew? She wondered briefly how much more Martin MacNab now knew, and, as on another occasion, whether luck or character was fundamentally responsible for the part Martin MacNab was continuing to play in the life of the Hut. In so many lives, in one death, she thought sadly, not numbly, without realizing the change. She had no time. The SMO had gone on to repeat a conversation concerning Henry Weaver's career that he had earlier with Mrs Weaver. Being a good physician he never forgot a 'special' nursed an individual as well as an illness, and the more she knew of the human being, the better she could understand and nurse him or her.

'Legal civil servant when war broke out whose first-class brain already had marked for the reserved list. He got shunted into some hush-hush branch, evacuated far from London, and spent the war decoding or doing whatever such chaps do in their backrooms. Speaks half-a-dozen languages. Brilliant chap, but after the war packed it all in, moved back home and into this Arumchester firm. Born in his present house. Father was a solicitor. Dead now, but according to Mrs Weaver never got over the shock of producing such a brilliant son. Double first.' He looked from one to the other. 'In my experience, none so stupid as the academically brilliant. Hopeless at applying common sense to the normal hazards of life. Chap's a born countryman. Should know his own soil. Matter doesn't cross his mind. I'm never sure what specifically founds such stupidity. Mental arrogance or mental myopia.'

'Combination of both.'

'You think, Sam? H'mm. Yes. I'll accept that. Well, Nurse Carr – he's all yours, pro tem. I need not add –'

'No, Dr Evans, and thanks.' She smiled slightly. 'I'll hope not to haul you back, but –' She left the sentence unfinished and all three touched wood.

For the rest of that night she had no more time to think of MacNab, or the obvious misconceptions that had evoked Mrs Weaver's hostility towards her. Last night she had even less time for such thoughts and only saw her patient's wife when looking at her asleep between the curtains of SW1.

Mrs Weaver went to bed at half-past eight last night. The full shock was hitting her and a combination of exhaustion and wishful thinking convincing her Henry was a little better. He had slid into a light sleep shortly before eight, and she thought him deeply asleep and for the night. It was one of their marital jokes that once off he was out for the night; it was another that he liked sleeping flat on his back. She was sure it was because she had told this to that rather nice old bod Sister Flo, that Henry's bed had been enlarged; she was equally sure he must be getting better tonight and that the only reason why Sister Flo, or that quite nice little Nurse Mason (the day-special, normally the Florence staff nurse, who was an inch taller than Caroline and two years her junior), or that terribly nice Dr Lincoln Browne, hadn't told her so, was not to raise her hopes too prematurely. Yet they had to see that Henry was smiling a little in his sleep. Only a little smile – but lovely to see – and she was so tired that now she knew he wouldn't miss her, she might as well have an early night and miss having to see that smug little trollop – poor Martin – what fools men were – poor, poor Marigold. Such dears, both of them, and simply wonderful yesterday.

Marigold was always wonderful; always pretending she didn't give a damn about Martin's popsies. 'Who expects a perfect husband,' Marigold once said before the war, 'but what would we do without ours?' They had found out in the war. Year after year of blackouts, rationing, queuing, short-ages, coping alone with babies, toddlers, the house, the garden, always alone, always cut off by petrol-rationing even from the next village and tied down by children; always sleeping alone except on the precious few nights when your husband got home and was usually too tired to do anything but sleep. No fun, no parties, no cosmetics, no fashions, nothing much to eat but stodge so you put on weight, no glam uniforms, no kudos, just pressing on, year after year with nothing but bad news on the wireless and those wretched government posters telling you to DIG FOR VICTORY, AVOID CARELESS TALK, SAVE THIS – SAVE THAT, BE LIKE DAD KEEP MUM and the children as soon as they could talk asking 'Where's Daddy, Mummy?' and so-called friends looking at you in that nasty way because Henry wasn't in uniform. 'Aren't you lucky Peggy! How did he swing it? But he's so clever – and such a joy for you to know at least your husband's safe.'

Safe! If they'd only known – but she hadn't either, till it was over. Not even suspected. Until that night last year, months after he had come home and started in the firm, and told her. And she had told him that whatever he had done, or did, she would never divorce him, and that she never wanted to talk about it again, and then she had cried all night alone in their double-bed and he had slept in the spare room. In the morning she told him, 'It's not just that I don't believe in divorce. I love you too much. Now, shut up and go to work. What do you want for supper?' The only person she had ever told about this was Marigold, and she had said, 'Of course you did. All that ailed Henry was the war. Knocked all the men for six. Come and help me pick raspberries. . . .'

She still couldn't think of that night without weeping. She couldn't bear to go through anything like that again, or have Marigold suffer it – and she had never seen the look she saw in Martin's face when he put down the receiver in their hall yesterday morning. Just for a second he had looked a different and a haunted man, and now she had seen his trollop she knew exactly why. Just as, since a little after Christmas, all Ash, all Bread Street, had known why, until the snow was too thick for the van and he had had to use the tractor, 'Mr Martin's' van was often temporarily parked in some side-lane near the hospital. 'Always been a bit of a lad, Mr Martin, same as his dad and his granddad, rest their souls. . . .' All Ash, all Broad Street, but not Marigold, or she would have told her. Henry had forbidden her to tell Marigold. 'I know I've no right to talk, Peg, but. . . .' Typical man! Men always stuck together. But now she had seen the trollop she was glad she had kept her mouth shut to Marigold. This time it could be serious. The trollop was so damned pretty and slim and such a smug little fraud creeping around looking so damned virginal in that grey dress, white dog-collar, white apron – not a spot not a crease – and that monstrously attractive little muslin cap perched on her head. It wasn't fair – it was plain indecent – that she should look like that and good, sweet Marigold as if she had been pushed through a bush backwards and needed to start banting. Why, why, of all the nurses in this hospital was she Henry's night nurse – or had she pulled a string? Yes, of course! She wanted Henry on her side and was bound to have all the doctors eating out of her hand – Oh no! Not all! Dr Lincoln Browne never even bothered to look at her when he had to say something to her. She was getting no more change from him than she would from Henry. He was very fond of Marigold. 'In Martin's terminology, salt of the earth. She loves him for what he is and not for what he's not, and what he is when not behaving like a retarded snottie (midshipman), is a very fine chap.'

No, the trollop would get no change from Henry. His partners all said he could read a client's face faster than he could do *The Times'* crossword, and that never took him more than a few minutes. He'd have her number. . . . She sighed and slid into sleep.

She did not wake until a day junior came in with a cup of tea. 'Good morning, Mrs Weaver. Your breakfast tray's waiting for when you want it.'

'Oh, God – must be after eight! How's my husband?'

The nurse was very young and looked innocent. 'Oh, Mrs Weaver, I'm just a first-year pro. I'm afraid its no good asking me. No one tells me anything,' she lied with the self-possession of a staff nurse.

A few minutes later Sister Flo came in looking very kind, and to Peggy, very old. 'I'm glad you had such a good long sleep, my dear. I'm sorry to have to tell you Mr Weaver is not quite so well this morning.'

'He suddenly went downhill in the night? Why wasn't I called?'

'There was nothing sudden about it, my dear. No occasion to disturb your sleep. The slight deterioration was only to be expected at his present stage as it is part of the course of his illness. Nurse Carr recognized this. She nursed it in the late war, most fortunately, as such previous experience is invaluable to patient and staff, and since, as you have been told, the condition is now rare, she happens to be the only young trained member of our nursing staff with such experience. This is why she has been sent to us from the Theatre Department. I would not normally trouble you with such a purely staff matter, but I hope the knowledge will provide you with a little extra reassurance. Ah, your breakfast! Thank you, nurse! Take your time, Mrs Weaver, dear, and when you are ready I will take you in to your husband. Then, later this morning, Dr Fenton will be in and he would like a little talk with you in my duty-room. I shall be there and we will have a nice cup of tea.'

'Couldn't I just look in before I eat this, Sister? Just for one minute?'

'He's having a little rest, dear. You wouldn't wish to disturb him and gentlemen so like seeing their wives all prettied up. And when you do go in you will find your chair a little back from his bed. I know he's appreciated having you to hold his hand, but for the time being, better not to touch him.'

'Not even kiss him good morning?'

'Blow him a kiss, Mrs Weaver, dear. He will understand.' Another nurse had appeared. 'I shall be with you directly nurse. Forgive me, dear, I have to leave you, but I shall be back.'

The nurse was holding up one of the front curtains and Peggy saw behind the girl the tall, dark-haired, impeccably neat figure in a long white coat and the fear that had been gripping her since Sister came in, nearly choked her. She now knew the morning medical rounds started at nine; it was only half-past eight, so they must have sent for Dr Lincoln Browne for Henry! She did not know that on this occasion Sam had not been sent for, but having just met Caroline on his way to breakfast and her's to 'supper', he had come here first. He had gone when Sister took her into SW3 and after one look at Henry she had been thankful her armchair had been pushed so far from his bedside that he could only see her face if he turned his head. It took her a little time to realize that now he could not turn his head, and that the little smile she had thought so sweet was fixed on his face but not reaching his eyes that were only half-open and had an odd stare. She sat very still, breathing carefully, leaving her knitting in the knitting-bag on her lap, watching Nurse Mason taking his pulse every few minutes, giving him little sips of some drink through a straw in the spout of a china feeding-cup every few minutes, crooning softly, 'Just another little suck, Mr Weaver, that's the way,' as if Henry were a baby and not her adored, brilliant husband of whom she had always been so proud until – no – what did that matter now? What did anything matter now but Henry – darling Henry – oh God, why have you done this to him? To me? This is the worst moment of my life. . . .

She was wrong. She discovered that in the duty-room when old Dr Fenton in his black jacket and pinstripes sat by her in the two hard chairs at the duty-room table, Sister Flo stood by her other side, and Dr Lincoln Browne leant against the closed door and folded his arms. After Dr Fenton's gentle, lucid explanation, he said, 'You have been most courageous and co-operative, Mrs Weaver. We know you will continue to be both for your husband's sake. It distresses me to have had to tell you all this, but you had to know what to expect. That is your right as next-of-kin and we would be failing in our duty to you – and to your husband – not to uphold it. Now, I think perhaps, Sister – ah, thank you, Sam! I'm sure Mrs Weaver will find that cup of tea most refreshing.'

They had let her go back to Henry, but never for long. Some nurse kept touching her arm, beckoning her out, and only beyond his curtains, murmuring, 'Your lunch-tray is in the duty-room, Mrs Weaver'. . . . 'Your tea-tray is waiting in the duty-room, Mrs Weaver.' She had not been able to swallow more than a few mouthfuls, though she was so thirsty that she drank cup after cup of tea. Then this evening, not long after she got back from 'Your supper-tray is waiting in the duty-room, Mrs Weaver,' that again she had barely touched, Dr Lincoln Browne and the curly haired boy in a short white coat whose name she had forgotten but whom she liked for the cheerful smiles he always gave her, had come in together. They were standing by Nurse Mason between her chair and Henry's bed when the boy had suddenly turned, touched her shoulder, jerked his curly head for her to leave with him and all but pushed her soundlessly across the now dimmed corridor into the duty-room before vanishing, but not before she had seen his face had stopped looking boyish. It could have been a minute or an hour later that two student nurses had carried in the armchair, then Sister Flo had come in and asked her to sit in here 'For the time being, dear'. She had found her knitting and handbag in the chair, and put both on her lap when she sat down to wait, praying for Henry, praying for someone to come in and tell her what she dreaded to hear and Dr Fenton had warned her might happen. But no one had come, until now. She had to talk – even to her.

'I've got to wait in here as I think he – he –'

'Yes. I've heard. I'm very sorry.'

'How've you heard?' She snapped in acute anxiety rather than hostility. 'You've just come on. Haven't got your things off.' She gestured accusingly at the cloak, greatcoat and shawl Caroline was hanging on one of the wall-pegs as was her prerogative, being a staff nurse. None of the Hut wards had nurses' cloakrooms. The student nurses used the pegs on the inner wall of the clinical (urine-testing) room further down the outer corridor that in all Martha's wards was called 'the flat'. 'You haven't had Sister's report yet!'

'No. But I've just been talking to Dr Lincoln Browne outside.'

'Oh.' She was too fraught even to think. 'You're wasting your time with him, my girl! I – I suppose you all tell each other things.'

Caroline concentrated upon removing her watch and pinning it in her bib pocket. 'Hospitals are like villages, Mrs Weaver. I know. Raised in a village. In both the grapevines go non-stop and everything gets embroidered to make a better story. But we weren't swopping grapevine gen outside. Just the latest medical report on your husband that I was very sorry to hear.'

'Has – has he had one of those – those muscular spasms that Dr Fenton said might develop?'

Caroline looked up slowly. 'I'm afraid so.'

'Oh – yes – I was afraid – but no one's told me and – I've been waiting – waiting –'

'In hell. I know.' Caroline glanced again at her watch. It was five to nine and irrespective of professional situations Sister Flo objected sternly to the night staff's appearance at her desk in the main ward for the handing-over report at ten seconds before or after nine o'clock. 'You do know why you've been asked to sit in here?'

'That's obvious. To get me out of the way.'

'Yes, but there's more to it.' She paused for quick thought. As you're convinced I'm MacNab's popsie, nothing'll stop you hating my guts, but if ever anyone had a reason for not thinking clearly it's yours now. But I think you want and need to get this clear and have the guts to take it – if you believe me – and as you're in sheer hell there's a chance you will. She said briskly, 'I'll tell you the rest, but I'll have to talk fast as I'm due on in a few minutes. Anything you don't follow or want enlarged, ask me later. Okay?'

Peggy Weaver gave a long shuddering sigh of assent.

'Right. Just one more question. Did Dr Fenton explain what these spasms are like?'

'He said – very – distressing.'

Being a honey, he would, honey, thought Caroline. Understatement of the year. 'Very,' she said, 'to suffer and watch. And, too often, once a patient goes into a tetanic spasm, another can be brought on by the smallest unexpected sound, the smallest current of air – like a tiny draught or just the clink of a cup on a saucer – either can provide the physical stimulus that sparks off a spasm – I've seen both do it and –'

'I wouldn't have moved or uttered –'

'We know that. You've been marvellously quiet. Only, he would have known you were there. He's loved having you there. He told me last night. He was so pleased you were having such a good sleep that it helped him to get a little more sleep. That's true, Mrs Weaver, not patter.' She was firm. 'Yes, his sedatives helped. But they aren't knockouts and can't be as he's having them regularly.' She left out 6-hourly for his first twenty-four hours and since 4-hourly. 'He didn't have a good night last night, so every bit of sleep was a vital bonus as again – this isn't patter – sleep is the best medicine. And the runner-up to sleep is peace of mind. So their throwing you out just as he was going into spasm this evening spared him the extra agony of knowing what watching him in one would have done to you. He can't control his body, but his thoughts are his own as neither the sedatives, analgesics nor the toxin of tetanus are clouding his mind.' Once more she left out, and the way tetanus leaves the mind clear until the terminal stages is one of its most terrifying effects on the patient. She went on, 'Another reason for chucking you out, was to spare you. Yes.' She raised a silencing hand at the unspoken interruption. 'We know – of course we know – you've been in hell since Friday and that no matter how much we wish it, we can't haul you out of the pit yet. But we can try to avoid pushing you down deeper whenever that's possible. Only, always – always – first we have to think of and for your husband. He's our patient. The patient always comes first, everyone and everything else, second. Isn't that how you'd want us to put it?'

Peggy Weaver nodded dumbly. Caroline checked her watch. 'Sorry, must go, but before – quickly – your husband's my third patient with tetanus. Both my others went into spasm at this stage and both later walked out on their own two feet. Please God Mr Weaver'll prove how often events come in threes. Sorry. Must go. See you later.'

Peggy Weaver stared into her lap and made no response. After another look at the distraught, downcast face, Caroline left the duty-room without another sound.

The only sound in SW3 was the sound of Henry Weaver's shallow breathing in a shallow sleep that owed more to exhaustion than medication. He looked as abnormally large and solitary as his bed. This stood alone in the middle of the small ward that was lit by the rose-coloured rays of the red, lined, shade-covered bedside lamp standing on one of the several bedtables that, with three glass surgical trolleys, were lined lengthways against both inner hardboard walls. The bedside locker was pushed back about a yard from the right bedhead;

directly opposite, about two feet from the left bedhead, were a black oxygen cylinder in a taller, black iron, low-wheeled, portable stand, and beside it on a low wooden stool, the round glass flow-meter through which the oxygen passed. The green rubber oxygen mask and tubing hung round the cylinder's neck; the water in the flow-meter was still as a stagnant pond; and the tall, thin, white pole, double-hooked at the top, towered up from the bedhead like a flagpost waiting for its flag. Early on Friday afternoon in the duty-room, Mr Henty had removed that pole from a portable transfusion-cum-drip infusion stand, and then, wearing a surgical gown and plim-solls and working as if pole and bedhead were made of egg-shell, so firmly fixed on the pole that it could only be knocked over if the bed itself went over.

The high white bed had all four foot-castors locked, and was extra-weighted by the fracture boards under its own and the cot mattress over the extension made by removing the top footrail. The cot mattress, loaned from Martha Ward, was sideways on, and made up with under mackintosh, cot blanket (another loan) and adult white cotton drawsheet. Generally when fracture boards were used under mattresses they were just lain in place. But every board and both mattresses were lashed to the bedframe with crêpe bandages; flattened bandages were more comfortable to lie upon than twine and crêpe was stronger than gauze.

Henry Weaver was just under six foot two and weighed fourteen stones. He had a strong-boned, humorous, clever face and fairish hair the night lighting turned grey and he lay in the only posture his body now allowed and he could tolerate. He lay outstretched on his back, a single soft pillow under his head and the arching of his back that tonight was much more apparent, thrust out his jaw and chest, and under the white, split-backed, hospital nightgown, knotted and hardened to a board his abdominal muscles, and so tightened those in his cheeks and mouth that now he seemed to be grinning in sleep.

On his first night, only the occasional hint of a smile, thought Caroline, standing alone at his bedside. He had been just awake when she took over half an hour ago and he had managed to swallow the four ounces of strongly laced glucose – 'lemonade' – she had given him before sliding into this shallow sleep. She was deeply thankful he had had the drink and was having the sleep, and, in another way, to have this time to study his unguarded appearance before he again woke and she had to control not only her expression, but her thoughts from the penetrating mind behind the unnaturally staring, half-open eyes.

Last night, she thought, more than a hint; and tonight the terrible gargoyle grin that was the *risus sardonicus* of tetanus. And standing, watching, touching neither the man nor the bed, as it was a couple more minutes before his next ten-minutes pulse and respirations rates had to be taken and recorded on the special P and R chart, the deterioration since this morning in the patient she had come to like and respect tremendously, saddened her as she had forgotten she could be saddened.

In Sister Flo's long, detailed day report that had heightened the chill in Caroline's bones, Sister said, 'Tonight, I'm afraid, Nurse Carr, the classic *risus* and *opisthotonos* (the arching of the back). Mercifully, the penicillin is keeping his chest clear. He can no longer tolerate the oxygen mask, nor, for the time being, can we risk slipping it on when he's sleeping and we've no tent for a man his size, or, indeed, any adult larger than a child. The nasal feeding tube had to come out. We got it in under light anaesthesia, but immediately it wore off, he began choking. We cannot keep him anaesthetized and no question yet of replacing it, or substituting a stomach tube. His heart is having enough strain. So we are back to all fluids by mouth. His muscles are too tautened and sensitive for a rectal tube. As for a drip – temporarily – unusable. If setting one up did not precipitate another spasm – as the physicians are con-vinced and I wholly agree – as great a risk that we would have the snapped off needle end lost in a vein. There it is, nurse. Get in all you can by mouth. I'll be in to see him before I leave and will have a word with Mrs Weaver and try and persuade her to have another early night. If, as I suspect, Mrs Weaver insists upon spending the night in the duty-room –' she looked at the night senior sitting on Caroline's right, 'make her comfortable with rugs, pillows and a foot-stool, Nurse Shaw. Thank you, Nurse Carr. I need not keep you for my main ward report.'

He was still in that shallow sleep and Caroline was making her third twinned entry in the P and R chart, when Sister Flo came soundlessly between the drawn front cotton curtains that in daylight were navy blue and nightlight, purple. Sister stood watching by the bedside for over a minute before putting on her reading glasses to look first at the P and R, then Fluid In-Take and Output, then the hourly Temperature chart above which was written in red ink: ONLY IF PATIENT AWAKE. On one of the bedtables on a small white enamel tray were oral and rectal thermometers in disinfectant in separate containers, (former fishpaste jars); from admission, Henry Weaver's temperature had been taken under one armpit – the safest method when every taking risked snapping the glass ther-mometer and the greater risk of the balls of mercury being swallowed, or inhaled or deposited in the rectum.

More charts; Dangerous Drugs; Schedule A drugs; Peni-cillin; Anaesthetics; and the two-hourly Blood Pressure now, with so much else, temporarily discontinued. Flush with a row of charts, the thickening file of medical case-history notes topped by the prescription sheet and dogclipped to a hardboard 'bedticket' normally hung on the lower footrail of the patient's bed. Caroline, handing each chart in turn, kept a constant watch on the sleeping man; between each chart, Sister lowered her glasses to peer at him over the tops.

Eventually she took off the glasses and exchanged with Caroline a look that seemed to give nothing away, but that so erased the thirty years between their ages that momentarily Caroline had the illusion that standing by her was a slight young woman with the great white wings of an Army cap framing her fair face, the scarlet folds of her shoulder-cape pinned back, the bronze star of Martha's pinned to the right top corner of her broad-strapped white apron bib, and the sleeves of her grey uniform dress upon which Caroline's was modelled, as neatly rolled above the elbows as her own now. Then she blinked, and the illusion vanished and standing by her, watching Henry Weaver, was old Sister Flo with, as Caroline, a bronze star on the corner of her strapless apron bib. Old Sister Flo, stout, starched, kindly, and given Flo that was normally regarded by the Hut as a sinecure, because she was nearing retirement and no longer had the physical stamina for running an acute ward, and was thought to find too confusing the many radical changes in treatments of so many conditions that were consequent on the new drugs either already, or sometimes it seemed monthly, coming into use.

Poor old Sister Flo, she's had it, said the Hut, and Caroline, to her present shame, had said it too in her general training. It's never dawned on any of us, she thought now, that the old girl's always known more about pure nursing than any of us, and she does. Her lamp isn't out yet. And though she doesn't much like the look of him, there is something about him that she does like. If I could ask her now, I know what she would say, 'Very disturbing, nurse, but, mercifully, he has not got the Look.' And Thank God, she's right, she thought. He hasn't got what all the old sisters call the Look and by it mean, the look of Death. None of them, none of us, ever use the word Death, but nor when nursing DILs do any of us ever forget whose presence is hovering near – outside front curtains – outside the three red screens used round DIL beds in general wards – outside a ward entrance. And when we sense that presence at the bedside, whatever our professed beliefs, that's when we start praying. And so do some of the men (doctors) – not many – not all – only a few – perhaps because though they are the ones that sign the death certificates, we are the ones that hold the hands of the dying and close the eyes of the dead. Alters the perspective, she thought, almost academically, glancing again from Sister to the dreadfully grinning sleeping face and for the first time since talking to Sam outside, mentally she breathed out just a little.

A few minutes later she was alone with her patient. It was only just after ten, but the silence of 'the flat' was the silence of the small hours and not that of the start of a busy night. It would be eleven before the SMO and residents off with him this weekend began their night rounds. Night Sister's had already started in Charity; shortly the residents on this weekend would begin theirs, and later Sam would do a second when handing back the medical side to Dr Evans. Miles of walking all day and half the night for the men; all night and every night for the Night Sisters, thought Caroline, after making the next P and R check and sitting to chart it on the seat of the polished mahogany locker that was one of the scores salvaged from bombed wards and sent down to the Hut. To use a locker seat was a special's prerogative that was only otherwise granted to nurses feeding patients.

His eyelids twitched. She rose quickly, clamping down with both hands her skirts to prevent the rustle. But the twitch had been involuntary and after taking his pulse to be sure, she sat down again, listening to his breathing and the silence from 'the flat' where the only overhead light on had in a red bulb. SWs 1, 2 and 4 were empty and in darkness, the front curtains of the first closed, those of the last two, open. At the far end from the ramp, the main ward doors were closed and their glass panels blocked from within by open red screens. On Friday afternoon the ward telephone had been removed from its wall-shelf just outside the duty-room, and Repairs and Works had extended its flex to take it into the duty-room and from then its use had been restricted to out-going calls. The day and night switchboards had been instructed to put all inter-hospital and outside in-coming calls to Florence through to the Office Sisters' office by day and Night Office by night.

'No bells must ring in my "flat", Mr Henty,' said Sister on Friday. 'But I must have in Small Ward 3 some form of electric bell that will make no sound when pressed and produce a quiet buzz in the main ward. Can you arrange this for me?'

Mr Henty sighed heavily. 'I dunno, Sister. I do not know what you Sister ladies will ask of me next. A quiet buzz, eh?

Ah, well. Have to sort it. I'll be back, Sister.' He was back in about one hour his plimsolls under one arm, yards of flex, a bell-push, and wood-and-metal contraption under the other. 'Got a nice quiet buzz for you, Sister. . . . Do you nicely, will it? That's nice. Shouldn't wonder if we not started something, Sister. What I say is, trouble about starting things is there's no saying where they'll end. . . .'

The duty-room and kitchen doors faced each other across 'the flat'. The kitchen door was a chink of white light with mufflers round both handles keeping it just ajar. On both as on every door in 'the flat' were SILENCE, PLEASE notices; on the outside of the ramp door was a huge hardboard notice painted and put up by Repairs and Works on the afternoon that Mr Henty told his charge-hand was one Friday he'd not forget in a hurry and more's the pity. That notice read: NO UN-AUTHORIZED ENTRY TO FLORENCE WARD IN ANY CIRCUMSTANCES: WILL ALL AUTHORIZED STAFF AND VISITORS PLEASE REMOVE BOOTS HERE AND MAINTAIN ABSOLUTE SILENCE IN THE FLAT: THANK YOU.

Her eyes ranged up and down the sleeping man. Up and down, from the unnaturally furrowed forehead, back-tilted head and over the whole body stiffened to a rod-like, slightly arched piece under the top bedclothes that fell free at both sides and over the foot of the bed and were as neat as if the bed were empty. The shallow fluttering breathing caused no more than faint tremors in the turn-down of the top sheet above his thrust-out chest. The powerful respiratory muscles were struggling to keep his lungs working, the powerful heart was struggling to take the strain, and the glucose he had just had was beginning to remove the yellowish-blue tinge from his face and lessening the black shadows strangely outlining his features when she came on. The antitoxin was struggling to neutralize the deadly toxin and given time – given time, it would. But the antitoxin had not had enough time to prevent this evening's spasms, or the unbearable agony of the pain when every muscle in the body went into spasm simultaneously and the most powerful of all muscles that were in the back, gained supremacy, jerking the whole body into a half-hoop that left only the back of the head and the heels touching the bed.

'At times in those few minutes,' said Sam on the outer door-step, 'only his heels were on the bed. I had his head and shoulders, Nurse Mason one hand on his pulse and the other holding the oxygen mask just above his face, Dick had his legs and we all had a full-time job keeping him on the bed and the bed still. His jerks had it leaping off its castors and shaking so badly that if boards and mattresses hadn't been tied on the lot would have been on the floor. We jammed our bodies against the bed to steady it, but if Sister Flo and a day nurse hadn't arrived at the double, the bed would have hit the wall, not just shifted the couple of feet it did. God knows how you'll manage if he has one when you're alone at night.'

'Four of us on. We'll manage. Go on Sam.'

'That's about it, except that his heart can't take much more. For God's sake, Caro, pack in the glucose. . . .'

She recalled the anguish in Sam's face and voice when he said that, but not how, in that moment, she had never liked him so much. Her mind was too polarized on professional matters for such personal intrusions. Then again Henry Weaver's eyelids flickered and she was at his bedside in the next second. The lids half-opened, and a small smile lit the staring grey eyes.

She smiled and spoke slowly, softly, 'You've had a nice little kip, Mr Weaver. Just going to take your pulse,' she warned before touching him awake, 'then how about another little drink.'

'Thanks – thirsty.' He could only speak in a whisper and the words were slurred by the stiffness of his tongue and clenched teeth. And the effort of two words slightly beaded his upper lip.

'Please –' She tucked back her watch and put a finger to her lips. 'No careless talk. Walls have ears.'

The old wartime maxims returned the smile to the staring eyes, '*Mea culpa*,' he whispered, intentionally disobeying, and she could have hugged him for his fighting spirit and sense of humour that was never far under his surface. Both would help him survive; everyone needed the first and most the second, as humour was a tremendous salvation.

She said smiling, 'I'll forgive you, but please no more nattering till you've had a nice drink of ersatz lemonade,' and in answer he slowly, painfully raised his right thumb. She had come to know that corny mannerism that was anything but corny when made by a man in his condition. 'Drink coming up on the double.'

Not the double, slow-motion, not touching jug, measuring glass or feeder with each other. This time she poured in eight ounces of the dispensary-prepared 'drink' that was loaded with glucose and tasted like very sweet lemonade. It contained no fresh lemons; these were still too scarce for the quantities he, and the Hut's other DILs, needed every twenty-four hours. When she put the straw in the spout, she slightly bent it, then more than slightly flattened the tip.

'I'm just going to get the napkin under your chin – that's the form. Now my hand and arm under your pillow – just up a little – okay? Fine. Now, the straw between your teeth –' This was difficult but she just managed to ease in the flattened tip. 'One suck at a time. Take it easy, Mr Weaver. No hurry. I've got all night.'

The little smile lit the stare and contained so much gratitude that her own eyes had the forgotten sensation of being sandpapered. 'Nice work, Mr Weaver. Keep it moving.'

He was very heavy and so stiff that she was tilting rather than raising him, but the tilt was just enough for him to swallow with difficulty, but to swallow. It took fifteen minutes, but he drank it all, and only when she had laid him back did she discover Mrs Ames, Sam and Dick Dunlop were standing watching from just inside the curtains.

They had been there for a few minutes and still waited silently for her to tell Henry Weaver that they had come in. He was more accustomed to her, and as they had just seen again, as so often on the last two nights, she had forged with him the strong nurse-to-patient bond that worked both ways and was never stronger than between a DIL and his or her night-special. Almost invariably the dangerously ill sensed their own danger and the especial accentuation of that danger in the small hours of the night when the resistance of the whole human race, in sickness or health, was at its lowest ebb. The comfort of the security afforded by the certainty that one weak murmur or raised finger would immediately bring the expected touch, voice, and 'I'm here. . . .' was very great.

When the three came forward, she moved to the other side of the bed and surreptitiously dried on the back of her dress skirt the still trembling palm of her left hand. But again the glucose was reviving him, and he was whispering a few words without his face sweating.

Mrs Ames said in her gentle placid voice, 'Just going to take your pulse, Mr Weaver and give you some delightful news. The thaw must be starting. Our icicles are actually dripping.'

Again the staring eyes smiled and slowly, painfully, the right thumb rose. And Sam, inadvertently seeing the expression in Caroline's eyes, reminded himself vehemently not to look at her face again tonight. He hitched up his stethoscope. 'Just going to listen-in, Mr Weaver,' he said bending over the bed in the same second that enough of the ice-casing melted for the upper half of a tall ash, killed by the cold, to topple free. The ash was in the portion of the wood directly behind Florence. The falling trunk was trapped by the trees below and did not hit the wooden ward. Only the thunderous crack echoed through every ward in the hospital – and very narrowly missed killing Henry Weaver.

9

'Oh, to be in England now that April's there!' Dick Dunlop
picked up the unfinished crossword he had left on the window-
sill of the Residents' Common Room to go to supper. 'Oh, not
to be leaving a cushy joint showing the signs and symptoms of
being run-down to beat old Nye to the draw.'

'Oh for the bloody innocence of my lost youth,' said
Hoadley, returning to his armchair and today's *Times*. 'This
joint may be a wartime anachronism, but its too useful to
Martha's, as it will be to Bevan, to close down as its bloody
here with all parts in working order which is more than the
old firm and half London's hospitals will be for a good few
years. We're only half-empty for the same reason as Arumchester General and Milden Cottage (Hospital). Snow's gone,
sun's shining, work on land's months behind, no one's got
time to be ill. Similar syndrome hitting London so convoys
are coming down half-empty. Every outdoor trade's back on
the job, working overtime, and when a chap gets back home
he wants his tea on the table and not the wife up the hospital.
She's in no hurry as the sun's getting her washing dry and
giving her the chance to get down to her spring-cleaning.
Spring-cleaning cuts down gynae queues as effectively as air
raids emptied the psychiatric clinics. Nothing like being
bombed to cure neurosis. But this quiet won't last. Never
does.'

'Never,' echoed Dr Evans from the depth of an armchair and the tattered paperback Western he had joyfully discovered down the back of the sofa before supper. Now, at opposite corners of that sofa were Sam, with yesterday's *Times* and Bob Tanner re-reading a Peter Cheyney. The two other housemen presently on-duty had gone to listen to the wireless in one of their rooms. The RCR wireless had only two volumes, deafening and inaudible. The latest batch of medical students that included Paul Dawson with another pair, as his first spell had been interrupted, had gone from supper to continue playing ping-pong and bridge in the Lecture Room that from the day of Pat Jones's death had, by unspoken agreement of the entire staff, reverted to its real name. Miss Yelton, Mr Mathers and Simon Phillips were now home on sick-leave after making uneventful recoveries from diphtheria, and upon this last Monday morning Henry Weaver had gone home to convalesce in the care of Dr Yardley and later return for a couple of follow-up clinics at varying intervals.

It was a Thursday evening in mid-April and from the beginning of the month the Hut had been having its quietest spell since it opened. On Thursdays, the residents on-duty over the coming weekend were officially free from 1 to 11 p.m. and normally lucky to get off by tea-time. Today, as last Thursday, they had been off from 1.30 and this afternoon Mr Chalmers and four housemen had gone on bikes to Pine Halt, then by train to Arumchester, to see *Brief Encounter* that was showing again at the Arumchester Odeon and all had missed when it first came out in the war.

Dr Evans was also off, but he had seen the film with his wife before they married, and, in any event, neither he nor Hoadley infringed upon their juniors' off-duty. Dr Evans was a naturally solitary man, who cherished his wife's company, and when he had to do without her, preferred his own. His hobbies were walking, bird-watching, reading Westerns and writing to his wife. This afternoon he had taken a long walk before writing to Mrs Evans, even though she always rang him at around 9.30 on his half-days. Usually then, the on-duty residents were snatching late suppers to the disapproving sighs of Sister Dining-Room and mutinous looks from her staff, the others out, and the Evanses had the rare chance of a conversation only overheard by Frank on the night switchboard. No prospect of such privacy tonight, reflected Dr Evans, glancing at his watch and noticing Sam doing the same. Far too early to contemplate a night round. Nearly thirty minutes before the night staff were on; no man was more unpopular than the man seeking to get his round done early on a quiet night before the night staff had time to hear the day reports, settle their patients and Night Sister embark upon her first round. However, there was many a worse fate than enforced inactivity when the alternative was unnecessary and one had to hand a rattling good tale one hadn't read.

Only another half-hour, thought Sam, more than contentedly. If the 7.35 from Arumchester was on time, it would be in in the next few minutes and the jeep would have her back by 9. She would have to be on the 7.35, as the next, and last on weekdays, the 10.15, was too late for her or the flicks-goers. Nurses returning from holidays had to report back by 10.30 and off-duty residents by 11. The RCR overlooked the drive and he had chosen his present seat for its view of the open gates. Only another half-hour and he would see her again. He looked quickly down at his paper until his heart-rate and respirations returned to normal.

For these last ten days Caroline had been in Devon on ten days holiday made up from one of her annual three weeks with, tacked on, two nights off for specialling Henry Weaver and the one she had had owing. It had seemed to Sam ten months, an illusion unhelped by the sudden slackening of the Hut that had coincided with the arrival of a spring as glorious as the winter had been hard. All day, every day, the sun had shone from a cloudless blue sky; every day the sunshine had been warmer, turning the months of snow into old legend, filling the woods with birdsong, the clapping of wood-pigeons' wings and the ceaseless rustle of belated nest-building.

The setting sun had dropped behind the hospital hill whilst they were at supper leaving behind the kind of English spring evening he had neither dared recall nor hoped to see again when a POW. The wide country sky was a gentle powder blue, the first evening star palely glinting, and the soft pastels of the lingering, lengthening twilight lent a pink tinge to the grey bricks of the Lecture Room now front-edged with green and splashes of white. All the buildings facing the drive and Casualty Yard had narrow front flower-beds, and now in all, as in every garden in Ash, and the station-master's prized flower-beds lining the platforms and both sides of the little booking office at Pine Halt, the tough little wallflowers, that had survived months under the snow, were sturdy green clumps soon to flower, the massed spikes of the first daffodils were coming up, and clusters of snowdrops were flowering. Over the whole countryside lay a cobweb of young green that to Sam looked brighter and more exquisite every time he looked upon it. At every look had returned his wonder at seeing it again. He had been back in England for last year's spring, but he could not remember it, as in that period – as Caroline had once guessed – he had still been in the delayed-action shock of his release. But this year, he was not only back alive but back to life, and able to rejoice at the beauty and the wonder; and with the coming prospect of her return and the happiness that just to see her now provided, he was so acutely aware of his own joy, that from old, conditioned habit, he thought – easy, cobber, easy. . . . Too bloody bonzer – watch out for the booby-traps . . . they'll be there. . . .

As for Peggy Weaver on Monday morning. 'Isn't this weather perfect, doctors! Isn't everything perfect!' she exclaimed, when arriving to collect her husband and drive him home in his own car as Sister Flo was escorting from the open-doored main ward the morning medical round, done, as usual, by Dr Evans, with Sam, and Mr Bennet, the SMO's house-physician, in attendance. The duty-room door was open, and Henry Weaver, whom the round had already seen, rose from the armchair and came out to greet his wife. His clothes were a little loose, his face was a little frail, but he stood straight and took his wife's arm from affection, not for support. After more farewells the couple left together. The little group of staff, joined by Nurse Mason and the senior student nurse, watched in the sunshine from just outside the open, notice-less, ramp door, Henry Weaver walking slowly, but steadily down the side and on to the main ramp. He turned smiling. 'Wish I'd a camera. Wouldn't have to ask any of you to say "cheese".'

Sister Flo, looking years younger, said briskly, 'No need for a camera, my dear Mr Weaver. We shall remember you as you are today!' She blinked rapidly, then went back inside with the two nurses and Sam saw Nurse Mason fall behind to mop her eyes.

The three physicians strolled on down the main ramp and when they reached the stretch running by Casualty Yard, by special permission parked against it was the Weaver's elderly Morris Oxford and the couple were standing with the Deputy Matron. Henry Weaver turned back to draw Sam aside, 'Do me a favour, doc. When Nurse Carr gets back, tell her how sorry I am to miss her today. She knows the rest, but I didn't know quite what this day would be like until today. Thanks, again. All the best.' He returned for another exchange with the Deputy Matron unaware his wife had overheard his aside. But Sam had seen the glance her tearfully happy eyes shot her husband, and he thought again how rare an element in human nature was gratitude and how common, not just in the un-imaginative, were the blinding blinkers of prejudice.

The Deputy Matron waited to salute the departing car with a regal wave, then announce that this was a moment of great satisfaction for St Martha's, but, alas, time and tide waited for none and she knew the Senior Medical Officer would forgive her continuation of her morning round of all her wards. Dr Evans bowed his response and after she left, murmured, 'If one subscribed to a belief in miracles, one would have to chalk up two. One single, one collective. *Vide*, the single.' He nodded at the old black saloon turning slowly out of the main gates. 'The collective, that upon my return from London on his third night I was not immediately informed of four staff coronaries.'

'L.B., Bib Ref! "Total abstainer." Nine. R-something.'
'Rechabite.'
'Huh? Fits! How do you do it?'
'Parson's grandson, Dick.'

This was true but had no connection with Sam's having become, through Dick's passion for crosswords, the residents' recognized Biblical expert. One of the very few books he had had in captivity had been the small, battered Bible given into his keeping by the then Senior British officer a few hours before he died in April 1944. Sam had watched him die, closed his eyes, and helped bury his body, being one of the handful of prisoners with the strength to lift a spade. In that month the always endemic dysentery had flared into a major epidemic. After his release he had sent the Bible to the dead man's widow in England; her letter in return had reached him in an Australian hospital. 'I am so thankful it helped you and thankful for you in every sense,' she wrote, 'and perhaps one day we shall meet. I hope so, but for both our sakes, perhaps not for a few years. . . .'

He had not pretended to her, or to himself, that Bible had changed his life, but that its intellectual interest had helped save it he would swear under oath. But he remained incapable of voicing to others, this or anything else about the prison camps, and although the old nightmares had stopped, the jaundice faded, he had put on another stone and his face almost looked his real age, he stared unseeingly at the Lecture Room for a good five minutes before the emaciated, jungle-sored face of the long-dead Lt Col. disappeared from his mental vision and the raw edges of memory receded into a dark, locked, secret place.

'Why wasn't I educated?' wailed Dick. 'Latin, now. Six and ten: "collective title Roman senators". *Patres* something?'

'*Patres conscripti*,' growled Hoadley smiling. 'Should've got that, lad.'

'Sir, help much appreciated, but would Sir kindly spare salt in wound of one with only three weeks freedom between him and two years hard.'

'Hard?' Hoadley's booming laugh jerked Sam back to the tranquil beauty and hopes of the present without disturbing Dr Evans' concentration. The Sioux war-party had just spreadeagled the hero over an ant-heap and were waiting in ambush for the surviving remnants of a troop of US 7th Cavalry, galloping up in a dust-cloud. 'Good God, lad! Life of an MO in the peacetime Army's a piece of cake. Just remember three things. Penicillin for the clap; iodine for the ringworm; and if you slap a PUO, NYD (Pyrexia of Unknown Origin, Not Yet Diagnosed) on the nervous breakdowns to give the poor young sods a few days to dry their tears in general beds, odds on you won't have to bung 'em over to the psychiatrists.'

Bob Tanner looked up to drawl, 'If one may ask, sir, does the entire British Army suffer from gonorrhea, the *epidermophyton inguinale* and Lack of Moral Fibre?'

Hoadley just looked at him for the few seconds it took Dick to study the ceiling in gleeful anticipation, and Sam to reflect that Tanner had one of the most advanced cases of the Deprived Banana Syndrome he had come across since returning to England. There had already been a fair amount about last year, when he privately diagnosed and named the condition. Much more prevalent now and likely to reach epidemic proportions by the 1950s when all too young for the war would have emerged into adult life with anti-war – but not pacifist – chips, the size of the Rock of Gibraltar. He had noticed it was hitting both sexes, but his own the worst and inevitably. War had an innate attraction for schoolboys ignorant of the realities of warfare. Those boys had had to watch their older brothers, relatives, friends, and often fathers, having all the fun of climbing into uniforms, getting posted overseas to get into the killing, or be killed, or mutilated, or rot in prison camps, whilst they had had to slog it out at school. In day schools, boarding schools, their own or other peoples' homes in 'safe' areas; in universities miles out of the range of enemy bombers; or joints like this that had never heard one bomb go off, though in one of the most frequently used flight paths and, according to local legend, a regular recipient of unexploded bombs shed by the enemy aircraft beating it for the Channel and the safety of France. And what had the poor kids had out of it all? Nothing but safety, and no bananas, then the final insult; our side won without them. Never forgive us, thought Sam sardonically, never. And he too waited with amusement for what was coming.

'No, boy, no.' The ominous gentleness of the growl jolted Dr Evans from ambush and ants. 'And that –' the gentleness ripped off, 'you stupid, arrogant, young sod is precisely why you are now lounging on your lazy backside in a white bum-freezer and not a slave-labourer in Germany or decomposed stiff. War's not yet been over two years. For the last five you've been old enough to handle the rifle only your undeserved luck in having a father willing and able to educate you in medicine forced some luckless young sod to tote on your behalf. Nothing wrong with your health, is there, boy? Right. If you want to keep it that way don't exhibit such damnfool immaturity again when I'm around.' The claxon ringing of the telephone bell diverted him from Tanner's puce face. He stood up. 'Too early for your ever-loving, Evan. Probably David Chalmers for me. He said he'd ring from the station to say they were back in Ash.' They heard Dodds hurrying for the telephone. Hoadley paused to peer over Dr Evans' shoulder. 'Not to worry, old chap. Troops get him before the ants.' He turned to the door as what could have been a fairly near clap of thunder coincided with Dodds' 'Gawds truth!' at the sudden pain in his right eardrum.

'7.35 to Pine Halt, miss? I'm sorry, miss,' the guard consulted his turnip watch, 'been gone three minutes and forty seconds. Have you come in the Basingstoke that's running twenty minutes late and missed your connection? I am sorry, miss, but its a wonder to me some of our old engines keep going at all.'

'That's for sure, guard.' Caroline put down her suitcase and dropped upon it the scarlet beret that had come off in her race from a mainline to a side platform of Arumchester station. She smiled at the guard who wore his pre-war guard's uniform with the smartness of an ex-RSM of the Arumchester Yeomanry. 'Any hope of a taxi to Ash?'

He took his time. She was worth more than the second look, he reckoned, and for all her ladylike voice, if she'd been Lili Marlene she'd not have had to stand waiting under any lamppost. 'Best be honest, miss. Any lad with the petrol for the sixty mile round-trip won't be too happy blowing it on the one fare. Do better for himself saving it for short fares, but – no offence, miss –' he glanced discreetly at the blinding polish of his shoes, 'if any young lady could get a lad to use it on just the one fare, I'd reckon you could.'

She laughed, 'Thank you. I'll give it a try. If I'm not in Ash by 10.30, I'll get torn off a strip.'

'We can't have that, miss! You have the –'

'Do forgive my interrupting.' A woman appeared beside them. She smiled apologetically at Caroline and the smartly saluting guard. 'Don't tell me, Mr Treeves! I've missed my husband and the 7.35.'

'I'm sorry, madam. That you have. Mr MacNab stepped off the London and onto the Ash.'

'He would. When he went up to visit his mother today we didn't know I'd have to nip into Gilland for the fodder Jim Peters couldn't deliver as his big-end's gone.' Gilland was a village two miles from Arumchester. 'I've now to beetle back to the Halt,' she added to Caroline. 'I couldn't help overhearing you just now and if you don't mind a bit of corn –' she gestured at the fragments of dried fodder clinging to her old navy reefer jacket, jersey and slacks, 'can I offer you a lift in my van?'

'There now, miss, your luck's in!'

Caroline's gratitude concealed her interest in finally meeting this woman who was reminding her of a scruffy, voluptuous, Mrs Ames. And she thought, one more I owe Henry Weaver.

She had nursed Mr Weaver for his nine nights on the DIL that he had been taken off at 6 a.m. on his tenth morning. By then, Peggy Weaver had had her first night at home since his admission. On Caroline's last night Henry Weaver had been strong enough to talk more than throughout his previous eight during which period, just occasionally, he had whispered in delirium. On her last night his voice had returned to near-normal. . . . Remarkable woman, Marigold MacNab . . . only daughter of the Archdeacon of Arumchester, married at 18 straight from finishing school, no secretarial, business, or farm training, but when her father-in-law died in '40 – heart attack – she took over and handled everything from War Ag bumf (War Agricultural Committee directives and forms) to crops, milk yields, Land Girls and the few aged chaps she had left, as if born to the land. . . . Showed the same acumen after her mother-in-law's stroke – and though her own parents were then dead, used her clerical connections to get the old lady out of a chronic ward in Arumchester into a bed in a first-rate establishment run by Anglican nursing sisters not far from your own on the Thames but that proved infinitely luckier at missing all Jerry dropped around. . . .

They left the station together talking of the weather, the problems of petrol-rationing and train engines overdue for scrap-yards. In the station yard was a smallish, battered van with a high front cab and tarpaulined back loaded with fodder sacks. 'Not locked. Never is. Everyone knows our van. Watch out for your silk stockings climbing up.'

'Won't hurt 'em. Nylon's tough as hell.'

'Nylons! You must be in the money! Six quid a pair on the Arumchester black market. Really, tough? How long've you had that pair?'

'Eight months.'

'No kidding? I must get a pair – not that I'm often in a skirt. My God, could I use your long legs.' She heaved herself into the driver's seat, then sat sideways. 'Look, this is absurd. I'm sure I know you having heard so much about you from the Weavers and my husband. You must be Staff Nurse Carr. Marigold MacNab. How do you do?'

Specialling Henry Weaver had done much more for Caroline than get her this lift. She smiled, 'Yes, I'm Caroline Carr. How do you do, Mrs MacNab? Have you seen Mr Weaver since he was discharged?'

The joy in Mrs MacNab's smile was charming, and to Caroline, revealing. 'Yes. Managed to nip over to Bread Street this afternoon. I was about to ask if you knew he was home?'

Caroline's smile had widened. 'Heard yesterday. A buddy wrote me a postcard Monday afternoon. Whole Hut en fête and Sister Flo needing new size in caps. Marvellous news!'

'Just great!' Mrs MacNab put in the key and switched on. 'Must cast off and will you mind piping down till we're shot of Arumchester. All the cyclists drive me round the bend.'

'Same here. Can't bear nattering when driving in towns.'

'Something else we have in common,' said Mrs MacNab, not, Caroline registered, as Mrs Weaver might have said it, but exactly as Prue Ames might have done whilst smiling one particular placid smile. She looked with even greater interest at the chubby, cheerful, determined and very sensual face whose strong outlines were softened by the dishevelled fading blonde pageboy bob falling forward over her ears.

. . . She's turned Widdington into one of the most prosperous and largest farms in the county. . . . War Ag's pin-up for years for many more than the obvious reason for any pin-up – if there had been more young Mrs Martin MacNabs, they've said, this country wouldn't have had to be so dependent on its convoys of food from the States. . . . Martin's a very lucky chap and knows it. . . .

Very probably, thought Caroline, too engrossed even to remember to look at the cathedral. He likes – and after his hellish war – deserves to enjoy life, even if the more she's boosted his bank balance, the more she's dented his male-provider's ego. So he has to keep his eye roving to provide his own boosts and also, I've a hunch, re-kindle her interest. Now I've met her, I'm afraid he's had that, – and that Peggy Weaver should be thanking heaven fasting that a divorce would wreck her husband's career, and force Mrs MacNab to lose her children. She's no more the type to abandon her young than Martin the type to give them up. Nor would he, or any man, give her up without one hell of a fight. She's loaded with SA and brains. It's the first that's hooked her husband, the combination Henry W. on the rebound . . . oh, God, what a mess. Not her fault. When she married at 18 she was not seeking independence or a career; the war forced both upon her; she then had either to grow up fast, or go under. She did the first just as all those that could; those that could not have since turned into the types that pride themselves on never changing when the real reason why they have not changed is that they have not matured. They've clung to their immaturity in self-defence – and any man doing three years on the Atlantic run needed whatever self-defensive mechanism he could produce. Poor Martin – and poor, poor Pat Jones. She was as much a war casualty as any that came out in the lists.

She looked round the dusty, worn little cab and shivered as if at the touch of a dead hand. She stared into her lap thinking of the long dark shadow of the war that was still lingering and was likely to do so for years, wrecking hopes and lives as efficiently as it had now turned Europe into a grave-yard. She was so absorbed, that when Mrs MacNab next spoke, she was surprised to find they were in a winding lane miles out of Arumchester and that on the skyline ahead were the three wooded hills bronzed by the soft clear twilight.

'Henry Weaver and my husband say you saved Henry's life.'

Caroline blinked at the abrupt announcement. 'No, Mrs MacNab. Your husband did that.'

'To be honest, I think so too. Generous of you to say so. It was you that got Martin to bulldoze Henry into the Hut.' She paused a moment. 'How well do you know Martin?'

Caroline looked at her profile. 'Very little. We've only met twice.'

'So he told me.' Her tone was genuinely casual. 'I was livid with you for making him bulldoze me into getting the boys and me injected against diphtheria. I'm passionately against shoving dangerous germs into children and I hate needles – but I had to forgive you after we heard one of your nurses had died of it in Badgers' Heath. Upset Martin no end. He's so soft-hearted, I don't know how he survived the Navy. He nearly went round the bend when Henry was on the danger list. But isn't it wonderful he's done so well?' Her warm voice shook slightly. 'We're all terribly grateful to you all for what you did for him.'

'Just our jobs, but thanks all the same. Lovely to be thanked.' And not by 'all', recalled Caroline. Peggy Weaver had neither thanked, not said goodbye to her.

'Martin nearly went round the bend with joy Monday morning when Henry rang us from Bread Street. Widdington spliced the main brace!'

'My grandmother and I, yesterday.'

'Good show! I'll tell Henry tonight. I'm going to take Martin there after picking him up. Cheer him up. He's always a bit down after seeing his mum. Stroke, poor poppet. Dotes on her, naturally, being an only and a son. He tries to get up on a Thursday whenever possible, as its usually our quietest weekday, but sometimes he has to make it Wednesday or Saturday. Not Tuesday. Market Day.' She did not notice Caroline was again preoccupied by her own thoughts. 'Martin hasn't seen Henry since he got home. Couldn't spare the petrol till this afternoon,' she laughed quietly, 'when it so happened that the wife of one that shall be nameless needed real eggs for the wedding cake she's making her daughter – so this job now has a full tank! I say – that thunder?'

'Sorry. Didn't hear.' Caroline unwound her side window and stuck out her head to look up at the cloudless, powder blue sky, the first star, the birds flying in pairs towards the wooded hills, and then at the young green cobweb lying over lane verges, banks, and the empty fields. 'Not one cloud. Glorious evening.'

'Isn't it? I must be hearing things – oh damn!' A sharp crack had come from under the bonnet. 'I'm not hearing that! That's our swine of a fan-belt! Been due to go weeks and our last spare as we're still waiting for a new one. Hell and damnation!' She switched off, coasted to a stop on the nearside grass verge and jumped down into the lane. 'I do not understand the internal combustion engine.' She heaved up one side of the bonnet. 'Do you?'

Caroline had joined her. 'Depends what ails it. Yes. Your belt's gone – dropped? No, I think I see it – let this cool a bit and I'll fish.' She took off and dropped her tartan coat on the grass, then pushed up the sleeves of her black turtle-neck jersey. 'Let's see.' She dived carefully between the still hot parts and held up the badly worn, snapped belt. 'This one's had it.'

'Hell. So've we. Still nine miles to the Halt, Ash has the nearest garage, Widdington the nearest phone – and that's a seven mile hike and I hate hiking! But –'

'Just hold everything, pro tem.' Caroline looked at her legs then all around, and heard in a memory that for the first time seemed to belong to another young woman in another lifetime, the gentle Southern drawl mimicking the Yankee 'when a dame's gotta do what a dame's gotta do, sure as hell, babe, you start the action. . . .' She nodded to herself, kicked off her pre-war black brogues, unhooked and took off her stockings. 'One may do the job. Spare'll be handy, in case, in case.'

'Huh? You gone crackers?' The query was not impolite but as if it provided the only rational explanation.

Caroline laughed. 'Stick around and we'll find out. I've seen this done, but never done it before. Being nylon and tough, should get us to Ash. Let's give it a try.' It took over fifteen minutes and several attempts to fix on the makeshift belt. 'Try the engine.'

Two minutes later they were back on the road.

'Where did you pick up this handy wheeze?'

'Ambulance driver in the war.'

'You had nylons then? You must've had a Yank boy-friend.'

Caroline was about to hedge when she found it was unnecessary and that the physical removal of her final gift of nylons had somehow sprung the final lock upon her self-imposed bondage to the past. All over now, she thought, and so much was good and is good to remember, with gratitude for having lived, and yes – and so often laughed through it. 'I hadn't nylons then. Battledress trousers, long-johns, and mens' socks and a pair of their nurses' boots scrounged from the Yanks.'

'What were you doing amongst Yanks?'

'In a small British medic unit on temp loan to their 3rd Army.'

'When?'

'Late December, '44.'

'You weren't in the Ardennes show?'

'Briefly.'

'My God, you've been around! How did the wheeze come in?'

'After that show was over. I was in a convoy taking Yank wounded back to one of their field hospitals where a lorry was waiting to take our lot back to our own side and the fan-belt of the ambulance I was in packed up. No spares around, but our driver knew the nylon trick and that his buddy in the back had on him the pair he hoped would get him a week's bed-and-board in Paris on his next leave. Driver strong-armed pair from buddy.' She smiled reminiscently. 'I mean, strong-armed. Hand-to-hand combat in the road with our wounded yelling encouragement and laying bets and MPs going berserk as we were holding up half our own convoy and the one behind. Driver was the bigger guy, and won on a knockout. Cheers from wounded, bellows from MPs, whilst one helped our MO heave buddy into our back, driver did his stuff on the fan-belt and we got moving. Buddy recovered uneventfully, and later that MO told me that buddy never forgave

driver for those nylons – not the knockout – what's that between buddies? – and the driver spent the rest of the war
watching his back far more nervously than his front. But he
and buddy got back Stateside in one piece.'

Marigold laughed. 'Good show.' She glanced sideways.
'How about the MO? He a Yank?'

'Safe home Stateside.'

'Good show.' She glanced at her watch. 'Twenty past nine.
Not so good, but not to worry. Dora's baby-sitting tonight –
she's Tom Ford's daughter – and by now Martin's bound to
have rung and Dora given him the score. He'll guess I'm
coming from Arumchester and settle for a natter and smoke
with Bob and Charlie – station-master and stooge. Martin
never minds hanging about when he can natter. Loathes being
on his own. Odd that for an only, but big farms are chummy
places. Always someone else around.' She changed down
against the rising gradient. 'I've got to go over your hill. I'll
drop you off on my way down.'

'Thanks a lot,' said Caroline, suddenly profoundly grateful
that this interesting and disturbingly illuminating journey was
nearly over and to be returning to the Hut. She had not missed
it until yesterday when Sam's postcard and news had made
her so ecstatic that at supper her grandmother had insisted
upon opening her last hoarded bottle of pre-war champagne. . . . Nonsense, darling, of course I can open champagne! What do you think I would have done if I hadn't
known how to after your grandfather died and before your
father was old enough to tie his own shoelaces. . . ? Yes, of
course I want it opened. When a celebration is called for, I
like to celebrate and if we don't finish it tonight I've no
objection to a glass or two of flat champagne for elevenses.
Glasses, darling, glasses. . . !

The lane ran tortuously up the steep east face of the hospital
hill and, some fifty yards from the top, curved round the southern shoulder where the only passing place was cut out of the
hillside. Caroline, glancing from the passing place to the crest,
thought of the old footpath running up from behind Flo, and

Pat Jones's liking for 'pottering up the hill alone to get away from the hordes'. She sighed silently and sadly.

The bends restarted on the descent, temporarily straightened parallel with the Hut, then re-wound on down to the side road to Ash. They were still on the shoulder when Marigold peered forward. 'I smell smoke. Can't see any from the bonnet. Can't you smell it?'

Caroline reopened her window. 'Cordite?'

'Could be someone going after wood-pigeon – no!'

They had turned westwards and saw above the blocking high banks the upper half of a distant column of thinning black smoke smudging the darkling powder blue sky like a broad smear of charcoal. 'Some poor Ash bod's house on fire! Hell! The only fire engine for both villages is in Bread Street. Martin's created for years about Ash not having its own.'

'Is it from Ash? Looks closer.'

'Hard to judge when visibility's so clear. If you're right, could be Ash Manor. It's the only house between Ash and the station – poor old Dentons.' She half-smiled wrily as the bend forced her to crawl the van downhill. 'Not exactly Ash pin-ups. They bought the Manor last year when they returned from the States. They'd beat it there in the summer of '39. Martin swears they spent the war shedding crocodile tears and singing 'There'll Always be an England' – but they aren't bad types. If it is the Manor, damned bad luck, as the daughter they left behind to finish in college is due back in England tomorrow. I'll step on it once I hit the Ash road. Bound to need help.' The lane had straightened. She slowed to a stop a few yards short of the main gates, keeping the engine running. 'Can you cope?'

'Sure. Here – the spare in case you need it. And thanks very much.'

'Thank you.' Marigold thrust the stocking into her reefer jacket. 'Be seeing you!' She drove off with one hand waving out of her window with the other.

Caroline looked from the disappearing van to the charcoal streak merging into the high sky. From her present level it seemed far more distant, yet so uneasily reminiscent that now she was in the open she was sure she could taste – taste – the hint of explosives in the clean, sweet, still air. Sure? Not just association of ideas? Knock it off! She picked up her suitcase, strolled the couple of yards to the opening, then stopped still.

It was only on or just after lighting-up time, but there were lights on where she had not expected and off where she would have from Sam's postcard yesterday. 'Med staff lotus-eating non-stop. . . .' Not tonight, Josephine, not tonight, she thought tensely. The Doctor's hut and Lecture Room were unlit and clearly empty; it was well after nine, but the head porter was in his lighted lodge. Other lights in and outside of Admin, the TD, the Path Lab, Stan Parker, Henry Vic, Hope – why? Hope's medical – and all along the main ramp. Cas.'s red light, dimmed by the white streaming from fixed open doors, with on either side neat ranks of empty stretcher-trolleys set with mackintoshed mattresses and neat stacks of grey blankets; and the Ash-Can was missing. (This was the only ambulance that belonged to the Hut and had been given the hospital in 1944 by the Friends of St Martha's-in-the-Country, a self-formed local voluntary association and its nickname by the staff.)

Her gaze swung back to the lodge and met the head porter's open-mouthed stare. He was an ex-Flight Sergeant and a sturdy, youngish, quick-witted Londoner. He flung open the window above his stable door to call oddly uncertainly, 'It's you, Nurse Carr?'

She rushed to him. 'Of course, Mr Tims. What's the alert? That smoke? The 7.35?' she demanded urgently.

He could only shake his head, then mutter, 'I – we – thought you'd bought it.'

She thought she had misheard. 'The train?' she insisted.

'Not like you mean, nurse.' He had to get his breath before going on and in the talkative stage that was one of the after-effects of shock. '7.35's no worse than a bit shaken. It just pulled in not more than the few minutes and passengers taking their time getting off seeing it don't go back to Arumchester till 8.05 when this old HE (high explosive bomb) goes up.'

She caught her breath. 'Where'd it been?'

'Buried in one of the flower-beds on the down platform since Jerry dropped it no one knowing when nor that it was there. It was, nurse,' he said grimly. 'Went up taking up half the platform and booking office. We heard it from here and poor old Dodds hasn't heard nothing since he took Mr Chalmers' first call just as it went up. I tell you, nurse, his luck was in.'

A tidal wave of emotions rendered impossible coherent thought. 'Mr Chalmers – ?'

'Gone to the pictures.' He explained this, rapidly. 'Like I says, nurse, Mr Chalmers's luck was in. He'd said he'd let the SSO know when they got back to Ash and had to use that box out the Ash side the station yard by the bike racks as some other poor bloke got first to that public phone on the wall by the booking office.'

A dreadful, intuitive guess pierced her confusion. 'Oh, God, no,' she whispered. Then, 'Go on, Mr Tims.'

'Well nurse, – the blast has Mr Chalmers on the floor, the housemen off their bikes, and all glass flying out the box, but mostly missed 'em, Mr Chalmers said. They picked 'emselves up and rushed back to lend the hand and after the quick, proper look, Mr Chalmers, he rushes back and gets through to the Ash exchange he doesn't know for how as the one telegraph pole he can see's snapped in half. Wires held seemly. Dorothy's on and she puts him through the Arumchester cop shop, then gets busy herself calling Dr Yardley and the Ash cop that lives in Bread Street same as the ambulance and fire engine. The Arumchester cop tells Mr Chalmers they'll be sending ambulances and engines from Arumchester, Milden and all over, but we've not heard any's shown up. Got to take time. Mr Chalmers wasn't wasting none. He gets back to the SSO for all the help we can send.' He shook his head grimly. 'Not as we're meant to send out, not being what's called a local hospital and it being Martha's rule Martha's don't send out staff. The SSO, he says they knows what they can do with that rule and the SMO wasn't hanging about, neither. Martha's got another rule, SMO says, Martha's looks after its own and aside from Mr Chalmers and his lot and he reckoned you and Alice (the Hope wardmaid) on that train, if Ash folk wasn't our own after all they done for us, what were they and seeing he's off – his half-day, see, nurse, he's off. Next thing you know, nurse, Dr Evans is driving the Ash-Can seeing Bill's taken the hospital van home for the night (Bill, the van and all-purpose Hut driver lived in Ash) with Mr Tanner, Staff Nurse Tilden from Hope, Nurse Kilbride from TD, six student lads and all the extra stores we bunged in the back in the ten minutes before they gone. The SSO and Dr Lincoln Browne had to stay being in charge the Hut and didn't like it, neither, I can tell you. They'll be busy, once they start coming in. Nurse Tilden rang back for the SMO to say they got there and whole village turning out to lend a hand and be needing treatment for shock theirselves, she says.'

She had turned numb. 'How many?'

He looked wooden. 'No one's saying yet, nurse, and from what Mr Chalmers said from what was lying about not easy to give proper numbers.' She shuddered violently. 'Yes. You'll know, nurse. But –' he hesitated, 'Mr Chalmers did say for sure four goners. One from his uniform, Bob Dawes, the station-master and one was our June's big sister –'

'Not June of the switchboard!'

'Seemly, nurse. Works – worked in Arumchester – hairdressing – and Charlie Mercer the porter as was on the gates and missed it put the name to her and –' again he hesitated, 'tell you straight, nurse – it was the other poor young lady as Mr Chalmers thought must be you – not from Ash, Charlie Peters said, so Mr Chalmers thought must be you but couldn't say for sure as – as – er –'

She said numbly, 'She got it in the face.'

He needed a deep breath. 'That's what he said, nurse. And seems she got your colour hair and down like you now and – tall, slim, he said – and wearing a sort of black-and-white – like your coat now, nurse – and seeing Sister Theatre said this morning you'd be back on the 7.35 and he couldn't see you among the survivors – well, you know what he thought, nurse, and – I tell you, Nurse Carr,' his voice shook badly, 'when I just see you walk in from the lane and take the long look – like – like you come back for the last look-see, I tell you honest, nurse, I don't know what I thought.'

'I believe you, Mr Tims,' was all she could say for the moment. It could so easily have been my ghost, she thought, and right now – now – I could so easily have been dead. If I had been, and it were possible, I would have wanted – longed – for just one last look – oh God. She closed her eyes.

Mr Tims looked at her drained, white face, then suddenly over her head. 'It's right, sir,' he called quietly. 'You're not seeing no ghost. It's Nurse Carr.'

She spun round to face Sam, standing transfixed about a yard behind her and looking greyer, older and more haggard and haunted than she had ever seen him. And staring at her as if he dared trust neither his eyes nor ears and was beyond speech.

She walked slowly to him and put her hands on his shoulders. 'I missed the 7.35 and got a lift from Arumchester, Sam,' but he did not seem to hear. She took his cold face in her hands, drew it down, and stood on her toes to kiss his lips. 'It's me, honey. It's me,' she said as they heard the sound of the Ash-Can's engine coming up the hill. Two minutes later Sam was back in Cas., and less than thirty minutes later she was back in theatre clothes in the theatre proper.

I O

'That's the lot, Nurse Carr.' Stan unhooked the ramp doors then reached for the greatcoat he had left on a filled cylinder. He had just carried out and stacked against the walls on either side of the entrance to await the morning collections by Surgical Stores and the Path Lab, a two-deep row of empty oxygen and anaesthetic cylinders and single row of metal 'milkman's' cages crammed with upturned, empty, glass blood vacolitres and plasma and glucose-saline bottles.

'Thanks, Stan.' Caroline looked up from writing at the duty-room desk. 'And for all your help earlier.'

'As well we copped it on a quiet night.' He looked over the finally clear and tidy corridor that despite the recent influx of clean air reeked of anaesthetics, ether, carbolic, cordite, cement dust, wet earth, and the cloying sour-sweetness of freshly applied plaster of paris and fresh-spilled blood. 'But for the hush might reckon war still on.'

'Well might.' They exchanged a long look. 'God knows how we'd have coped on a heavy night.'

'You can say that again, nurse.' He slapped on his old RAMC beret and told himself he was always a mite chilly afore dawn. He didn't swallow it. He knew more than the pre-dawn chill now had him cold as this last winter. Spent hours, he had, ferrying from the head with a dresser taking the foot, stretcher-trolleys from Cas. to wards, ward beds to and from theatre, and none with just a night junior as escort party. First lot, a houseman with the blood on the one side, the Cas. staff nurse with the drip on the other and both with their free hands holding steady the strapping keeping in the needles that Dr L. B. bunged in first go to veins so collapsed that no saying from watching how he done it. Practice, that's what, he'd told that young Dawson, one time they was whisking an empty back to Cas. And when time come for beds to go to theatre – L. B. hisself along with the blood and the day staff nurse from Stan Parker, or Henry, or Vic with the drip till midnight when Night Sister packs off all the day staff and takes over the drip.

Then, just after midnight, no escort party and seven covered stretcher-trolleys up the Yard and main ramp to the morgue up by the chapel. Poor stiffs got to go somewhere till coroner says what's what, he'd told the lad, and Hut got the handy, empty fridges. Hadn't reckoned nothing left to turn his stomach when he got his ticket. Getting old and gone soft, he had, he'd told that young Dawson, after they had to fetch up back of the morgue. The lad done all right for all he couldn't leave off over knowing No 4's face from last time he was down with his old mate as been one of the dips. Gone up the old footpath afternoon afore the last blizzard, he said, and seen the poor bloke and bit of fluff nipping out the old stone hut up top of the hill and down the side so sharpish they'd not stubbed their fags proper and seeing his mate wanted a smoke and they got none he got the one with the lipstick going for a few drags. Forgotten till he see's No 4, the lad said and couldn't leave off about it. Times a lad needed to talk to keep his mind off.

'Best see to my boilers, Nurse Carr.' But he hesitated, looking at her pale, tired, pretty face framed by the green turban and limp mask round her throat. Didn't do to think what yesterday been the face of a slip of a girl coming home the one day early. When your number come up it come up, and that's for why, he'd told that young Dawson. 'I – er – not had the chance, nurse, but – er – glad as your number – er'

'Thanks very much, Stan,' she said quietly and they exchanged a very guarded look.

'Right then. Best see to my boilers.' He wheeled away smartly and the ramp doors swung shut behind him and the silence returned to the mainly darkened, and, aside from Caroline, empty Theatre Department.

Not a TD tonight, she thought, a CCS (Casualty Clearing Station). A CCS better equipped, staffed and serviced than any she had worked in during the war. Only casualties identical; multiple fractures, varying internal injuries, multiple lacerations, omnipresent acute clinical shock; uniformly soaked in fresh and dried blood matted with ripped clothing, dust, earth, and glass and shrapnel fragments; uniformly visible the white splinters of bone sticking out of torn, bleeding tissues and through the filthied clothes only cut off under general anaesthesia in the theatre proper. And only in the anaesthetic room under pentathol, the faces properly sponged clean to expose the facial colour before the inserting of the laryngeal airways and fixing on of anaesthetic masks. The only colour in all the ageless, sexless faces, the grey-blue-white of acute shock and loss of blood.

But tonight, no shortage of instruments, dressings, blood, plasma, drips, morphia, penicillin, Anti-Tetanus and Anti-Gas Gangrene Sera. No having to work without X-rays, nor respite for the radiographer on-call who had arrived before he could be called, a few minutes earlier than herself. 'Picture of this, please, Mr Vincent. . . . Picture, please. . . . Picture this angle. . . . Picture here. . . .' Again and again for hours, the heavy portable X-ray machine swung and lowered into position, then the wet plates held up in turn to the portable, lighted screen, and later hung juxtaposed from the narrow white china shelves above the scrubbing-up sinks and transforming the hot, steamy, twin-tabled theatre into a surrealist photographic gallery.

Again for hours, Hoadley, dodging from anaesthetic room to theatre, bed to table, table to lighted screen, table to table, to and from the picture gallery. Occasionally grunting or growling some general observation, but more often silent and continuously demonstrating the experience, skill and talent that made him unsurpassed in the type of major surgical and predominantly orthopaedic first aid that could only be given under general anaesthetics and if given soon enough could save lives and the limbs that made those lives worth living for those that had to live them.

He had arrived from Casualty a few minutes before the first ward bed reached the TD and stripped off his blood-spattered white coat and tie in the corridor. 'All coming down in their beds, beds straight into anaesthetic room and then theatre, Sister. Whilst I'm tied up in here, Lincoln Browne's doubling for me outside. He'll send or bring 'em in in descending order of gravity and if one needs to jump the queue, it gets jumped. I'll need you and Nurse Carr to double as surgical assistants and instruments' nurses. Right?'

'Of course, Mr East.'

Never before in the Hut had anaesthetized patients been wheeled in their beds into the theatre proper and the removal of top bedclothes then exposed the grey Casualty blankets covering the injured in the clothes in which they had been carried from the ambulances. The innovation temporarily narrowed Sister Theatre's impassive eyes and widened the shocked eyes of Nurse Stevens (now Theatre 2), and the junior houseman and dressers that were all too young to have worked in Martha's, London during the war. There, as in innumerable other general hospitals in blitzed cities, by the end of the fifty-seven consecutive nights of the first London blitz in 1940, Martha's had learnt the benefits to the casualties of this form of treatment initially evolved from necessity; the in-rush of air raid victims had been too great to allow either the time or the staff to give the traditional pre-op blanket-baths, skin pre-parations and dressing in clean operation gowns for surgical emergency admissions; and then the results had proved spectacularly the value of touching such casualties as little as possible until either they were out of shock, or where im-mediate treatment was vital, only giving it under anaesthesia.

'One of the few good things to come out of the war,' observed Hoadley at one point, peeling off one pair of rubber gloves and getting straight into a fresh sterile pair. 'Right, Sister. Next in.'

From midnight at the second table, David Chalmers, two masks over his pale, scratched face, two pairs of sterile gloves on his scratched, scuffed hands working as steadily as if starting a morning's list after an undisturbed night's sleep. Bob Tanner assisting, tight-lipped and subdued behind his mask; John Bennett at the second anaesthetic machine, double-masked, but no gloves over his hands mottled yellow by the aquaflavine dabbed on after the superficial scratches and grazes had been cleaned-up and passed by the SSO. 'You'll do as second gasman – give Dick's schizophrenia a break. . . .' From then at the heads of the tables, the anaesthetists' heads swinging non-stop as a Wimbledon crowd from their patients' masked faces, to their machines, to the glass drip-connections set in the long thin red rubber tubing of the transfusion and infusion apparatus, and the third fingers of their left hands permanently on their patients' temporal pulses.

At midnight, Lindsay Kilbride, red-eyed, white-faced and furiously protesting was sent off-duty by Mrs Ames. 'Yes, nurse, I know the men have gone to the theatre, but Sister Theatre has Nurse Carr and Nurse Stevens, and will need you, her senior student nurse, back on duty at 7.30 this morning. Thank you very much, Nurse Kilbride. I hope you get some sleep.'

Finally, at 2.30 a.m., 'Thanks very much, everybody. These eleven are our lot, pro tem. They couldn't hang about. The other eight can and I'm not messing any about until out of shock.'

And when the men had left the theatre proper, 'Nurse Stevens, go and make the surgeons' tea, pour yourself a cup, and once you've handed in the tray, drink your tea and go straight off. Nurse Carr and I will clear and re-set . . . No, nurse! Once you've finished training, you too may stay on to clear up on occasions such as this. The prerogative of trained staff. You are down for a ten-to-one and I do not wish to see you back in my department until five minutes to one this afternoon. Thank you, Nurse Stevens. Off!'

Forty-five minutes later, 'If you're sure, Nurse Carr? Frankly, yes, I am a little tired . . . indeed I shall not take the morning off! Friday morning. SSO's list. However, possibly, our three 'cold' hernias may be temporarily postponed. You've got a ten-to-one and I don't wish to see you back until five to one. If we get another call in what remains of tonight I shall take it with Nurse Bell (Theatre 3) and inform the Night Office accordingly on my way off. . . . If you please, nurse, am I not Sister Theatre? Thank you – and for taking over the log and locking up. And – er – my dear, I am most devoutly thankful that – er –'

'Thank you very much, Sister.'

'Yes – er – well, goodnight – that is – good morning, Nurse Carr.'

The little travelling-clock on the desk held down a top corner of the back of an old temperature chart upon which the Night Ass. had listed the eleven names, ages, religions, occupations, addresses and next-of-kins of tonight's theatre patients and before entering each in the log, Caroline checked it with the name on the individual theatre notes stacked by the open log-book. It was 3.40 when she checked the last name, wrote it in the log, then before adding the long, detailed professional notes, took up the list to clip it to the sheaf and saw the shorter list that had been lying beneath. This had been put there by Stan at around 1 a.m. and she had first seen it a few minutes later when coming out to ring the Path Lab. All her old war-conditioned defences had then been up and intact, and she had thought numbly – not now – and made her call. 'Nurse Carr from theatre, Dr Sumner. We're down to our last two pints for Miss Alice Mabel Jenks . . . yes, our Alice from Hope . . . yes, she's the "rare". . . . You've two in hand and an Ash donor *in situ*? Thank you, doctor. Mr East will be relieved . . . no, no amputations. Mr East thinks he can save both legs . . . yes, singularly fortunate the Basingstoke was late. . . . Thank you very much, Dr Sumner.'

No urgent phone call that had to be made now. No appallingly injured theatre patients urgently needing her undivided concentration. No defences impregnable at this hour, after this night, and this evening, when alone in a silent department recording what had been done and, of necessity, reliving every moment.

She put down her uncapped fountain pen, and took up the shorter list. It included only one name she had known before tonight, and two more now known to the entire Hut staff. The first of those two had flashed round the grapevine before she heard it from Mr Tims, with the rider 'Our June's big sister – yes, our June on the day switchboard. . . .' The second, within five minutes of the final return of the Hut's rescue team at 11.45 with, 'poor girl was Carr's type . . . her cable from the States was telephoned her parents from Arumchester one hour after the bomb went up. . . .'

Reading slowly through the seven, numbered, alphabetically ordered names, she thought as she had not dared think since parting from Sam at the lodge – why them and not me? And those five words acted upon her defences like an underwater bomb on a massive concrete dam. At first, just a hairline crack and trickled escape of locked thoughts and emotions. Then her anguished gaze returned to the second and fourth entries:

No 2. Miss Brenda Susan Denton, age 22, C of E, university graduate, Ash Manor, n-o-k, father, Mr Robert Denton, S/A.

No 4. Mr Martin Alan MacNab, age 36, C of E, farmer, Widdington Farm, Ash, n-o-k, wife, Mrs Marigold MacNab, S/A.

The dam gave. The raging, roaring torrent burst through, overwhelming her with her first tears in years. She lowered the list blindly, and as her handkerchief was in one of her dress skirt pockets, pulled off and used her mask, and then the front of her gown skirt. When at last the torrent had swept away and the lake was still, that part of her gown was soaked as the discarded mask. And she was too emotionally exhausted to obey more than national instincts and her training.

She got up, rinsed her face under the cold tap at the hand-basin, half-filled and plugged in the kettle and when it boiled made tea in a cup with the last half-teaspoon of the TD's tea-ration. Then she went back to her chair, made a memo for Sister saying she had used up the tea, and sipping from the cup in her left hand continued writing with her right. Once finished, she re-read all she had written, then signed and timed it, 4.10 a.m., closed the book and replaced the shorter list under the clock as Sister Theatre had not mentioned seeing it.

She sat back in her chair, looking at the list, thinking deeply, grieving deeply for the dead and for the living that tonight had scarred, some with scars that would be visible for life and others with invisible scars that would last as long. That the pain of such invisible scars could dwarf all other pain she had long known but refused to envisage as it would have hurt too much. But the torrent had swept away with her defences her old, desperate need for a bulwark against reality. Ersatz protective cover for the ersatz, she thought, knowing she would never again apply that term to herself, nor forget how, after coming physically unscratched out of a world war, tonight, very easily, she could have been wheeled in a bed into her own theatre, or her mutilated body on a shrouded stretcher-trolley up the main ramp to a morgue in a converted Army hut. She had always known and again refused to face what her death would cost her beloved grandmother and brother, but she did not turn from that now, nor from how, this evening, she had seen with absolute certainty, what it would cost Sam – and herself. I would have known this last before, she thought, had I been looking in the right direction. I had glimpses when I was specialling Henry Weaver, but I wouldn't let myself recognize them, as I was too scared of being hurt again. I wouldn't risk it, and rationalized it, as being too scarred, but scared was the right word. It was only this evening that I had to see that in peace, as in war, the greatest of all risks is life itself, and the greatest of all tragedies, is the waste of life.

Hoadley had come in so quietly that she did not know he

was there until he addressed her from the open doorway. 'All post-ops just about satisfactory. Other eight picking up. I'm scrubbing this morning's list – probably do it Monday – and will see Sister later this morning about this afternoon's emergency list. Probably start 2.30. Sister gone?'

'Yes.' She made another note on the memo pad – the customary dogclipped stack of strips from the blank backs of old charts. 'You finished?'

'Yep.' He looked at her downcast tear-stained face, lit two cigarettes together, then handed her one. 'Shove it back if anyone comes in. Won't be the first time I've been seen with two going.'

'Thanks,' she inhaled gratefully. 'Not that anyone's likely to show up now Stan's gone and this joint's off-limits to all but you.' She looked him over in weary wonder. He stood square and solid, normally untidy, and limp-coated though he had put on a clean when he left the theatre, his heavy face was more grave than tired, and his shrewd, deep-set eyes clear and very kind. 'Sorry I can't offer you tea. Just used up our ration.'

'Not to worry. Just scrounged the best cuppa I've had since I can't remember when from Prue Ames in the Night Office.'

Her mind returned to the thoughts he had interrupted. 'You mean, since March '45?'

He scowled, but didn't pretend to misunderstand. 'Always said nothing like a near-miss for putting new life into a bod.'

'And for demonstrating the folly of procrastination. Plenty of time, I thought, peacetime – take it slowly – plenty of time.' She shook her head. 'Don't bet on it, Hoadley. Do I go on?' His silence answered her. 'Listen, honey, Prue's a pro's pro and the best nurse in Martha's. Of course she's always known that if anyone could have saved Hugh's life, you would have. And, God – did she see that again tonight and then offered you the first cuppa – isn't it? – that you've had from her since taking over as SSO.' He nodded slightly, still scowling hugely. 'Man, if you can't recognize an olive branch when you see one, see someone about your myopia, stat!'

He said nothing for several seconds. Then, 'Good God, Caro, if you'd bought it this evening, I'd have missed you like a cold bath. Useful things, cold baths. Bracing.' The scowl vanished and a small smile touched his eyes. 'Sam won't need 'em. He's last up and seeing some chap in William. I've just asked him why he forgot to tell me you and he were kissin' cousins.'

She looked at him quietly. She knew the Hut grapevine and its value as a safety-valve. 'Tims?'

He shook his head. 'Sister Cas, Nurse Mayhew, Dick and I were in Cas. with Sam when he beat it like a bat out of hell. Young Dick dropped the burnt feathers to open a book on the wedding date before the Ash-Can had its brakes on.'

'Figures. What did Sam say just now?'

'That even Homer sometimes nods and he had to see a chap in William. Let's have your fag.' He stubbed out and buried both in the nearest sand bucket. 'I need my bed.' But he turned and nodded sombrely at the list under the clock. 'Bloody awful show, but could've been a bloody sight worse. If those eleven had had to make the thirty-three miles over lanes and roads cracked and pitted by this winter, odds-on Arumchester General would have had not seven but eighteen BIDs (Brought in Dead). And had this been a normal night, we could've had more than seven in the morgue now. Prue's just told me Martha's, London have offered to send us help tomorrow. Just like the bloody Army. Always offering to post the reinforcements when the show's over.' He looked around the corridor. 'Something's got to be done about this set-up, but not tonight. I need my bed.'

'You do and you'll deal with, Hoadley. Sleep well, Mr East.'

He sketched an unmilitary salute and ambled out as quietly as he had come in, without saying more. She watched him go and when the doors swung shut, sighed a deep sigh that mingled sadness, gratitude, hope, and plain tiredness.

She had changed back into ordinary uniform and was pinning on her cap when she heard the knock on a pushed open ramp door and knew who was there before 'Lincoln

Browne, Sister. I've brought the provisional list for this afternoon the SSO forgot to leave just now. May I come in?' Sam requested as etiquette and a strict hospital rule demanded. Once a night list was over and the department was solely occupied by nursing staff the only men permitted uninvited entry where the SMO and SSO and as it was surgical territory, the former never used the prerogative.

She called back, 'Sister's off. Nurse Carr. Come in. With you in a second.' But she needed more than a second as her hands had begun shaking. She looked down at them as if she had forgotten she possessed them, then put on and hooked the collar of her long cloak before switching off the changing-room light on her way out.

Sam stood leaning on the desk copying Hoadley's scribbled list on to a memo strip. He had on his third clean white coat tonight and only the shadows under his eyes and blueness of his chin told the real time. 'Hoadley wants this one back.' He didn't look up. He was more tired than he looked for more than professional reasons and he had not known Sister had gone, but knew his own limits. 'I've just run into him again coming back here cursing blind at having forgotten this. I said I'd do it.'

'Thanks.' She moved to the other side of the desk watching him as if she had forgotten what he looked like. 'Why did William get you up? I thought there wasn't a medical DIL in the Hut tonight?'

'There isn't. William didn't shout. I was still up and wanted to check something I'd written in one chap's notes earlier tonight. On my mind and keeping me awake, I told the night senior.' He handed her the copy across the desk, pocketed Hoadley's, glanced at her unmasked tear-stained face, and pulled out and offered a half-empty, crumpled, blue paper-wrapped, packet of twenty Players. She gestured her refusal and when he lit up, though there was no current of air in the duty-room, the match flame flickered badly. 'She was so sympathetic I felt like Judas Iscariot.' He had to look back at her face rising like a sad lovely flower from the enveloping navy serge. 'These lights were still on. I had to see you again tonight and needed the concrete reason for hanging about up this end at this hour.' He glanced at the clock and then at the list below and his face tightened. He looked back at her slowly, and could not quite keep the pain from his eyes nor slight tremor from his quiet voice. 'Had your name been there, I couldn't have worn it, Caro. As you saw.'

'Yes.' She gripped the back of Sister's chair with both hands. 'I can't stop thinking – why them and not me?'

'I know the feeling.' He backed against one lintel of the doorway as he too needed the physical support. 'Ever since I got out – why the devil, me?'

She nodded, looking at him leaning there, looking a little too tired, a little too thin, but a tall, elegantly attractive man in his prime with the greying streaks just touching with distinction his thick dark hair, and remembering Hoadley telling her that when released from Japanese captivity Sam had weighed under six stones. He was then 29 and he's six foot one, she thought, and tightened her grip on the chair, and had to wait until she could control her voice. 'Probably a few hundreds if not thousands of your fellow POWs would have that answer, Sam. Plus those that missed out on dip this winter.' She looked deliberately down at the clock to make it clear she was straying no further upon his forbidden territory. 'I feel like Judas about never liking poor MacNab. He wasn't a bad type. Just a bit infantile, but basically kind, even when shooting lines or getting them crossed. He loved life and just wanted the world to love him. I suspect lots did. You liked him, didn't you?'

'Yes.' His breathing was back to near-normal, and her sensitivity, generosity and honesty were warming the cold, dark, secret places in his mind. 'I thought him an amusing chap in small doses, I always meant to buy him a drink one day. Least I could do after what he did for me.'

'For you?'

'Yes.' Their eyes met. 'Till he brought in his stockman and got you up that night, and I saw you and Hoadley in here,

I'd rather thought that you and Hoadley –' She was shaking her head. 'Yes, I do know I was way off target. Caught on some time back that Hugh Ames saw Prue Wells first – and Hoadley had to watch Hugh buy it.'

'That's the score. But –' and she told him what she had just told Hoadley. 'If things do eventually work out between those two,' she went on, 'in a way – a tragic way – MacNab again lent a hand off-stage. If he could know, I know what he'd say. "Bang on! Always happy to slip in the unwanted oar!" ' Her eyes were luminous with sadness. 'Like I've just said – very kind-hearted type. On our way from Arumchester his wife said he was so soft-hearted she didn't know how he'd survived the Navy. She said he'd been terribly upset about Pat Jones's death – not that she knew Jones's name, nor, I'm sure, connected those two. I've been sure you did, though you never told me. Right?'

'Yes. Didn't tell you as all I first had to go on I got from her when she was my patient.'

'Figures,' she said, thinking of his rare powers of perception, great compassion and professional integrity. 'Did the SMO say anything to you about Mrs MacNab?'

He inclined his head. 'He had to break it to her – he'd recognized MacNab – and he said she took it very quietly with dignity and guts. Then Mrs Weaver took her home to Widdington.'

'Mrs Weaver? She there?'

'Most of Bread Street and all Ash. The Bread Street types that had cars and petrol had packed them with volunteers and the rest came on bikes. Evans said that when he left all Ash was brewing-up, and no one's on their own in an empty house tonight. Mrs Yardley has moved in for the night to Ash Manor –' He saw her eyes clamp shut and moved quickly towards her. 'My dearest – I'm sorry –'

'Pipe down and stay put!' She jerked open her eyes and backed, raising an involuntarily defensive hand, and the gesture disturbed him nearly as profoundly as her kiss this evening. 'My darling man, for God's sake stay that side and get the hell out of here before I cry again, one of the Night Sisters looks in to see what's holding up the keys and not even Hoadley's writ nor your saving the Hut a dip epidemic will save your Martha's future!'

He had backed to the doorway as if dragged back by an invisible giant. He put his hands in his pockets and looked at her in a passionate, tender, wonder. 'Am I, Caro?'

'Yes. That's why I had to kiss you – please –' Her voice cracked. 'Don't hang about!'

For another moment or two he just looked at her in that same fashion. 'Not in here, my love. Elsewhere – *ad infinitum*,' he said with a determination in his low voice and thin face that had once astonished Dr Sumner. Then he was gone.

The ramps were empty and once more sparsely lighted when she locked the ramp doors. It was close to dawn, the moonless sky was imperceptibly lightening, the stars were growing distant, and over the black shadows of the wood above the hospital and the regimented line of nine long wooden wards hung the deep silence that immediately precedes dawn, when in the wild as in the wards, even the weakest, finally slept. And the night seniors told their juniors, 'Dawn soon. Get them through to dawn and whatever happens tomorrow, they survive tonight. . . .' In five wards the uncurtained windows reflected the gentle pink glow from the red night-lights, but those of Henry, Stanley Parker, and Victoria glowed crimson. Henry had five double-red-screened beds each with a red linen shade over the bedside lamp on the floor; Stanley Parker, six and Victoria, eight.

Caroline looked in turn at the three surgical wards, then walked silently down the ramp and into Casualty Yard, where now the only outside light was the red bulb in the coach lantern above the closed doors of the old Nissen hut. The Ash-Can was a greyish shadow in its usual parking place parallel with the darkened Path Lab. After handing in the keys at the Night Office, and reaching the side path to the Homes, she stopped to look back at the darkened Doctors' hut and saw

Sam's outline at the open window of his darkened bedroom. She had known he would be there, if he could; she knew he would always be there for her, when he could; and when he could not be there, she knew she would wait for him, gladly, and that they would both rejoice in the reunion, and their joy would grow with the years and their conversation would end only when the first of their lives ended and that the first seeds of their shared future had been sown in deep snow.

She waved and he waved back and stayed at his window watching her shadowy figure disappear behind the darker shadow of the Lecture Room. Then he turned away, put his old greatcoat over his pyjamas, and taking his cigarettes and matches silently left his room and went outside to sit on the cement steps running down from the front door.

He sat there for a very long time, smoking and thinking of this night and of other nights when he had sat on other hut steps waiting for dawn, when hope had been too dangerous to harbour, reality too dreadful for acceptance, and when he had known that physically he was scraping the bottom of the barrel and that all he had in reserve was will-power – and luck. Luck over all else, he thought, as when that ran out, you'd had it. No courage nor credit in having luck; just great gratitude for the buckshee gift. No discrimination about luck; it missed out on the good, the brave, the kind as often as it did on the other types, and too often, far too often, on the very best. No control over luck, just a varying measure over the use made of the gift. As for the gift of life, he thought, at last letting himself think of Caroline and the future with the kind of hope that until now he had never dared let himself entertain. From old habit, he waited for the mental caution ... easy, cobber, bloody easy ... but it did not come.

Only the gentle grey English dawn came up over the gentle green English countryside. And as he sat there watching in the greatest wonder and gratitude he had ever known, he heard the first voices of the waking birds and then all the birds in the woods on the three hills singing a glorious chorus of welcome to the birth of the new day.

To Sam, sitting there in his old greatcoat over his pyjamas, that dawn chorus was both a lovely requiem and an exquisite *Jubilate Deo*.